PRAISE FOR *SOU[...]*

'A beautiful reminder that music has [...]
told our story. This is the intriguing and playful story of music itself.'
— Zan Rowe, broadcaster

PRAISE FOR *WHOLE NOTES*

Ayres has achieved the extraordinary. In choosing to write about the
beauty of music, and life itself, he has created something gorgeous in its
own right. This book has an almost divine presence that reaches into
the reader. I am not a musician, or even remotely talented in the field,
but in this work I felt exposed to the sublime majesty of it all through
Ayres' talent, vulnerability and humour. This is a precious book,
overwhelming in its sensory evocations and more necessary than ever
in the current moment. — Rick Morton, author

With deceptively simple prose, Ed offers a truly beguiling account of
himself, intertwined with the miracle that undergirds everything –
the music that saved his life. The clarity on display in his writing is
memorable. — Geraldine Doogue, broadcaster

In this book, Ayres does so much. In seven chapters he extols the power
of music to offer us bravery, knowledge, resilience, kindness, wisdom,
hope and love. He writes in the same manner he speaks – with utter
grace … *Whole Notes* may appear to be about music, but really, it's
simply about how to be kind, and how to listen without judgment.
Which is the best definition of love, no?
— Jessie Tu, *The Age/Sydney Morning Herald*

This is a gorgeous read. It is entertaining and educating in equal measure, and will leave its readers inspired. — Celia Cobb, *The Strad*

Don't miss this book – it is an ode to music, by a truly inspirational teacher ... His beguiling style of writing is clear and honest, as though he is in the same room sharing his innermost thoughts with us, and one feels privileged to be there listening ... on every page his humour bubbles through. — Inge Southcott, *Loud Mouth*

Joyful and intimate, a delicately told ode to music ... He invites us to view the mystery of life on a large canvas of outstandingly gorgeous music. — Bishop Ian Palmer, *The Melbourne Anglican*

With his collection of essayistic reflections on the beauty of music and what the process of learning it can teach us about life, Ayres has gifted his reader with something truly generous and utterly joyful.
— Stella Charls, Readings bookshop

PRAISE *FOR CADENCE*
[Ayres'] passion for music is never far from the surface.
— Nick Galvin, *Sydney Morning Herald*

provocative, intelligent, surprising and funny ...
— Australian Arts Review

PRAISE FOR *DANGER MUSIC*
Ayres writes with forthrightness and compassion in this timely, powerfully told tale. — Fiona Capp, *Sydney Morning Herald*

Sound Bites

Ed Le Brocq

ABC
BOOKS

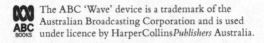 The ABC 'Wave' device is a trademark of the Australian Broadcasting Corporation and is used under licence by HarperCollins*Publishers* Australia.

HarperCollins*Publishers*
Australia • Brazil • Canada • France • Germany • Holland • India
Italy • Japan • Mexico • New Zealand • Poland • Spain • Sweden
Switzerland • United Kingdom • United States of America

HarperCollins acknowledges the Traditional Custodians
of the land upon which we live and work, and pays respect
to Elders past and present.

First published in Australia in 2023
by HarperCollins*Publishers* Australia Pty Limited
Gadigal Country
Level 19, 201 Elizabeth Street, Sydney NSW 2000
ABN 36 009 913 517
harpercollins.com.au

A catalogue record for this book is available from the National Library of Australia.

ISBN 978 0 7333 4308 7 (paperback)
ISBN 978 1 4607 1619 9 (ebook)

Cover design by Hazel Lam, HarperCollins Design Studio
Cover images by shutterstock.com
Internal illustrations licensed from iStock and Adobe Stock, or used under Creative
  Commons and public domain from Wikimedia Commons
Author photograph by Greville Patterson
Typeset in Minion Pro by Kirby Jones
Printed and bound in Australia by McPherson's Printing Group

to the musician in you

Contents

Invitation

Have you ever wondered where our music comes from?

How did we arrive here, a place where we can have a hundred musicians on stage executing the wildest rhythms, a singer performing the most heartbreaking of melodies, or a solitary pianist playing an instrument that weights half a tonne? How did the melodies and harmonies we are listening to today, right now, come about?

I'd like to invite you on a journey, a journey through a living tradition that spans millennia: the tradition of Western classical music. With this book we will roam its magnificently bendy path, from the Indus Valley to Mesopotamia, from the Ancient Greeks and Romans to mediaeval church music, from the Renaissance and the Romantics all the way through to music composed just last week by Australia's most creative minds. We will discover how notes from the Indus Valley influenced the development of scales by Pythagoras and his mates in Ancient Greece, finding their way through the Romans into church music of the Middle Ages and why some of those notes were banned. You'll find out how the invention of clocks changed rhythm, how pianos changed society, which composer was afraid of the number thirteen (and why we should be a little afraid of his music) and which composer had two skulls in their grave. We will investigate the development of instruments, including the human voice, from brutal surgeries and the liberal use of dried sheep gut to high-tech synthetic strings and instruments louder and heavier than ever before. And we will find out what some of the other fifty percent of people were doing with their music throughout history, not just the men.

Why is Bach's music so complex and hard to whistle and so perfect for our time, even though it's nearly three hundred years old? Why was Nannerl Mozart sidelined in favour of her younger brother? How did music grow from being a single line to a full orchestra and why has it gone back to a single line again? Is a piece of music that is just silence really music? And why does the horn point backwards?

This book aims to show you how and why, but it is a pocket rocket guide, so we will have a short ride in a fast machine — this is music history as you've never read it before. Together we will follow the highways and byways of our great music tradition, and when we arrive at the end, which will be music being written *right now*, I hope that you and I will listen even more profoundly than before, because this is *our* music. And with this guide, each note will tell its story.

1

Love songs, Ancient Greek–style

The year is 2240 BCE, the place is Mesopotamia and love songs are a big hit this year. Between the Tigris and the Euphrates, love songs are played on a gishgudi, a plucked instrument hung around your neck with a strap. Some things never change, not even the eyeliner.

And it's not just love songs and gishgudis that are in fashion: music is central to Mesopotamian culture and instruments are worshipped as demigods (you may feel the same about your guitar in the corner). God-like harps and pipes and cymbals are played in dancing songs and drinking songs, for weddings and funerals, for parties and for lullabies (well, maybe not the cymbals for the babies).

The first named composer in the world is Enheduanna, an Akkadian high priestess who writes music for Inanna and Nanna, the love/warfare goddess and god. Women composers will be silenced and ignored in centuries to come, but not yet. And Enheduanna is not only the first named composer we know

3

of, she is also the first named writer and poet. She writes temple hymns to be sung in call and response, a style continued through the centuries by Giovanni Gabrieli and his surround-sound music for St Mark's in Venice, as well as through gospel, hip-hop and rhythm and blues. In her temple in the country that is now called Iraq, Enheduanna has made herself comfortable, taken a reed stylus and a tablet of damp clay and carved her music into posterity; when musicians recreate this music, somehow those four and a half thousand years seem to disappear with the sound.

And this is where a trade ship sails into the port of music history.

Around the world, different cultures still use different numbers of notes in the octave: many Asian cultures use five notes (the pentatonic scale), and in Indian classical music the

octave is divided into seven basic notes, which can then be further divided into the subtlest of changes, twenty-two shrutis. Mesopotamians trade with the Harappans from the Indus Valley, and alongside precious stones, elephants and fancy furniture, comes music — players, instruments and songs. Who knows exactly how this cultural exchange may have influenced music history, but it must be significant because the Mesopotamians agree with the Harappan musicians and decide to also use seven notes in their octave. To this day, each of our music modes (structure of notes) has an equivalent in Indian classical music. Western music will continue to use the seven notes (the heptatonic scale) for the next four thousand years; it's also called a diatonic scale. Sounds fancy, but you know this sound already — it's the same scale Beethoven and Shostakovich and Lady Gaga will use in centuries to come. That's why 'Ode to Joy' sounds like a Mesopotamian pub song. There are not that many fancy terms to learn in music, but 'diatonic' is a handy one. Think Julie Andrews and her 'Do-Re-Mi'. It's a line of notes going up (and down again) where there are a mix of whole steps and half steps, or tones and semitones. And you know that sound as well — if you sing 'Happy Birthday to You', the first two notes are a whole step. Now sing the first two notes of the *Jaws* theme — that's a half step. There you go. Just mix a party song with some sharp teeth and that's your music theory done.

The culture of the Mesopotamians spreads through trade and travel, and now, around 800 BCE, the city states of Greece are using some of the same sounds and instruments — harps, lyres or kitharas and a pipe called an aulos made from bone or wood.

Now you might think playing the oboe is hard (according to *The Guinness Book of Records*, the oboe and the horn are the two most challenging instruments — what about the bagpipes?), but at least there's only one of them in your mouth at a time. With the aulos, you need to stick two between your lips. Yes, two, just like when you play two recorders at once to annoy your parents. And the two aulos (auloi) are different lengths, so they make different notes at the same time. The aulos is so hard to blow, the players need to use a leather strap around their heads to keep their face in one place and stop their teeth blasting out; unfortunately, this doesn't always work, and a myth is born of one player dying during a performance when his face explodes. Hercules plays the aulos. Enough said.

The word *music* comes from the Muses, the goddesses of literature, arts and science and music is played everywhere in Greece — for the military, the theatre, in temples and by students at school, although good luck getting a permission slip from your parents to learn the treacherous aulos. Speaking of school, megastar maths teacher Pythagoras works out that if the length of a vibrating string is halved, you get a note twice as high, and from that simple observation stems the way we tune our instruments in Western music to this day. Plato — yes, that Plato, of *The Republic* — also believes music is present everywhere in the universe; he calls it the music of the spheres, but we just can't hear it. (If Plato waits a few thousand years he will find out he is right: the vibration of earth is 7.83 Hz. That's a B flat, if you'd like to play along.)

If you like *Australian Idol*, you'll love *Ancient Greek Idol*! Aulos and kithara players compete in front of thousands of people for golden wreaths and jars of wine or olive oil. Perhaps not quite a Tesla, but if they win (and their face doesn't fall off in the process), they become as rich and famous as Guy Sebastian.

So some things never really change, and to hammer that point home, Plato vents about modern music in about 400 BCE, saying that if you have anarchy in music, you have anarchy in society: 'musical innovation is full of danger to the State ... when modes of music change, the fundamental laws of the State always change with them.'

You've got to hope Plato never meets John Cage. Or the Sex Pistols.

Athenaios Athenaiou, 'Delphic Paean', c. 128 BCE

It's certainly a challenge to recreate music from so long ago: two thousand years is a bit of a stretch when you may have trouble recreating something you wrote last week. Thankfully, many musicians and scholars dedicate their lives to this stuff, poring over fragments of clay, stone and papyrus looking for the tiniest of clues. So the next time you listen to the hits of 200 BCE, give a nod to the classics nerds — without them we wouldn't be able to listen to this music at all.

This song is composed around 128 BCE for a big festival in Delphi (think Glastonbury in sandals not wellies), and the hymn is usually played on the aulos and the kithara, the Gibson of the ancient world. The composer, Athenaios Athenaiou, clearly wants his music to last a while, as it is carved into two stones and positioned halfway along the Sacred Way of Delphi. Talk about an artistic statement.

How do these scholars know what the music sounds like, I hear you ask? Good question. They read the poem and infer the rhythm from the poem's metre; for the melody, the inscribed stones have the music notes chiselled above the words. Its order of notes is called the Lydian mode, the same as Raag Yaman in Indian music.

But what does it sound like? Strangely jaunty. But also like a child who is not getting what they want and goes on and on and on relentlessly saying the same thing, the same way, over and over, until they run out of breath and start crying. A bit like that sentence. So yes, as repetitive as minimalism, with a skipping rhythm that will have you wanting to pull out your jump rope. That crazy aulos playing the music sounds like a baby's wail (even though the poem talks about the 'shimmering tunes' of the sound … yeah, right), and alongside the wail the kithara thrums with a chocolate heartbeat.

Would you use it as a lullaby? Probably not. Would you whistle it at the back of class to annoy your music teacher? Definitely. And if they complain, just say it's the Muses in you.

2

Very plain, very chanty

Now that we know about those Ancient (they were young once) Greeks playing instruments where you can lose your teeth and using the Happy-Birthday-meets-*Jaws* diatonic seven notes in an octave, we can skip forward a few hundred years.

After the Romans have reused Greek music, stirred in some Persian influences and made it their own (think Abba remix in white togas instead of white jumpsuits), we have arrived in either the Mediaeval Ages (if your spelling is tops), the Dark Ages (if you're feeling pessimistic) or the Middle Ages (if you're between forty and sixty years of age and your middle is starting to grow). Also about 1000 CE.

Sure, you don't want to get a skin infection, break a wrist or have an eye operation, and you might get dragged off to fight in the Crusades, but the music is great. I should correct that: the folk music is great — down the pub, at festivals and weddings — but if you want cheerful music, do not, do not, *do not* go to church. There is only one unison line (the same note) of chanting in church music and the name says it all: plainsong, or plainchant. Very plain, good for napping.

But how did things get so … plain?

The very early Christian church borrows from Judaism the idea of singing psalms, and as you know from the previous chapter with Enheduanna and her hymns, the Mesopotamians were singing in a religious setting a while before that.

But why chant, or sing? Good question. Singing brings everyone together, and just like singing a song at a footy match fills the space (have you been to a Welsh rugby match lately?), early Christians need to bring their people together and fill their new basilicas.

Until the church bosses choose controlling their people over positive group dynamics, that is.

In an early example of music being used for control, an issue that will reverberate all the way through to the Taliban in the twentieth century, in 364 CE congregations are banned by the Council of Laodicea from singing in church because the church bosses *don't want any more bad singing*. Seriously. This is what the council writes: 'Besides the appointed singers who mount the ambo [big pulpit, not an ambulance driver] and sing from the book, others shall not sing in the church.' And with that the church service is taken away from the people and put squarely in the hands and larynxes of the priests, until Martin Luther comes along with the Reformation in the 1500s. That's over a thousand years of not being allowed to sing. It's the equivalent of the music teacher not tapping you on the shoulder in school choir auditions. For a thousand years.

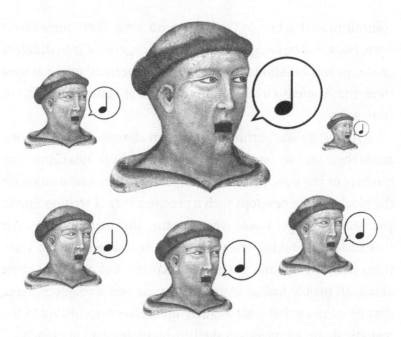

Around 600 to 700 CE, there is a split in the styles of chanting throughout Europe — Ambrosian chant, Gallican, Hispanic. In fact, the styles begin to fragment so much that church and political leaders are a little alarmed. With all these different styles, and sometimes languages, how can you know what people are singing and, most importantly, how can you control them?

Charlemagne, the newly crowned Holy Roman Emperor, sends singers from the Schola Cantorum in Rome all around his empire; a crack team of singing teachers to straighten things up and take back control, as only music teachers can. And the chant that wins out is the Gregorian variety. In an early example of questionable advertising, Pope Gregory says the chants are communicated to him by God through a dove. That's some clever dove, because the Gregorian chants are organised into different modes or combinations of notes that have been inherited at least from the Ancient Greeks and possibly the Harappans. So not from a dove.

And just as you're thinking you can change a note here or a mode there and no-one apart from those pesky Schola Cantorum teachers or the dove will notice, forget it. There's a new monk on the block and he develops such a precise a way of writing music, you need never get a note wrong again. This method is so clear that instead of taking ten years to train a singer, he can train them in one. His name is Guido of Arezzo. Before Guido came along, all people had to remember a tune was a rough guide of dots or neumes that went vaguely up or down according to the melody. A sort of melody-linked-to-bouncing-ball approach.

Guido does three things:

1. He adds lines so the dots have somewhere to sit.
2. He adds letter names to the notes (A B C D E F G).
3. To help with reading the music, he is the guy who gives us do for a deer, re for golden sun etc., he just doesn't do it running up a mountain in a lovely dress. He runs up a mountain in a lovely habit instead.

These inventions are as important to music as writing is to literature. And it's why we can now listen to music by the most performed and recorded composer from this time, Hildegard of Bingen.

Hildegard is born in 1098 in a little village called Bermersheim, close to the Rhine. The tradition of the time is for the tenth child to be tithed to the church, and as the tenth child, Hildegard is sent off to the church to be educated. You might think of an airy, sun-filled schoolroom and chapel, with the occasional frolic in paddocks with Julie Andrews. Not quite. Hildegard is enclosed in a cell, or vault, with her teacher and doesn't come out for seven years. Hildegard has poor health (perhaps it's the lack of fresh air), and her illness is now believed to have been severe migraines. Despite this, or maybe because of it, Hildegard has visions throughout her life, some of which may be the source of her music. She becomes a pre-eminent scholar of theology, biology, botany, natural sciences and music, even though women are barred from the priesthood and essentially silenced. Hildegard learns how to notate her music and she supervises the copying of it into a collection of parchment folios now known now as the Dendermonde Codex. You can see it today, either in person in Belgium or on the internet: the texture of the dried animal skin, the sear of the red ink, the vigour of the notes as they jest along the lines of the music.

Even though it is from a galaxy far, far away, chant sings its way into music to this day with Górecki and his *Symphony of Sorrowful Songs*, Enigma and their strangely addictive chant plus drum machine, and Björk and her off-kilter 'Ancestress'.

Hildegard of Bingen, 'O Sweetest Branch'

Hildegard of Bingen sits alone in her cell. It is winter and she has had her single meal for the day. Through her one small window she accepts the quivering light as a migraine begins again. She takes her quill, dips it in ink and starts to draw subtle marks on the parchment, marks which will sound for posterity.

The mediaeval fiddle, the ancestor of the viola da gamba and the modern violin, begins, a bourdon, or drone, sounding under the changing notes as a grounding for their flight. The fiddle's gut strings are pulled and pushed by the horsehair bow, a recurring image in manuscripts, stained glass and carvings of the time; the Mesopotamians worshipped their instruments as demigods, and now the fiddle or vielle is shown played by angels. Music is slowly descending to humanity. The drone of the fiddle dovetails into the incantation of a single voice; the sound is boundless, just as it will be in a thousand years with holy minimalism.

O tu suavissima virga, frondens de stirpe Jesse
(Oh sweetest branch, you bloom from Jesse's stock)

The music moves through the notes with a lithe step, mostly walking from one note to the next, sometimes taking a wider stride up, up, up to the escarpment of ecstasy and devotion. The music is intimate, resolute, calm, undeniable; a fragile light, shifting us to awareness.

Jesse's stock, or the tree of Jesse, is the first use of the image of a tree to depict genealogy. This music has similar progeny: here is a green root for the next thousand years of Western classical music.

3

Music and architecture, flying buttress-style

The year is 1163. It's early spring in Paris and King Louis VII and the Pope are in town, so it's party time because today they lay the foundation stone of what will be a consummate piece of architecture, Notre Dame Cathedral.

Music is sometimes called architecture in sound, and the construction of Notre Dame sits alongside the construction of a whole new sound in music: organum.

So you remember the last sound we heard, plainsong? Lovely as it is, plainsong is hardly cheering. Perhaps the musical version of a garden shed. Useful as garden sheds are, we may want to raise the roof a bit to fit in bigger tools, so as the cathedrals of Europe grow grander and more complex, so does the music performed in them.

Don't get too excited, though. What we hear added first is a simple drone, like the bourdon from the mediaeval fiddle. Think bagpipes rather than Dixie Chicks, because close harmonies are still considered overly manipulative and immoral, too racy for the church and therefore banned, but at least the garden shed is finally getting a window. The singers begin to experiment with moving the drone up and down with the tune in something called parallel organum. Sometimes the music is in parallel organum with a drone underneath as well. Very fancy. Now we have officially moved from monophony, one sound, to polyphony, many sounds. This is a big step for music, possibly even bigger than Madonna in the eighties.

As Notre Dame grows higher and higher and flying buttresses are added to support the height and weight of the walls, the music inside has its own flying buttresses. Singers begin to improvise more elaborate decoration over the main chant, mixing spaces between the notes, or intervals, until the music becomes so fancy and fast that people start to complain, thinking it sounds like street music (remember Plato and his complaints?). But once singers have sung this style, and more importantly, once it's written down in the new notation of Guido of Arezzo, there's no going back to plainsong.

Sorry, did you just sigh with relief?

Franco of Cologne, smelling pretty good and mates with some powerful knights, designs a way of writing notes to show how long they should sound. And speaking of notation, please welcome stage — sorry, *nave* — left two French composers, Léonin and Pérotin. Despite sounding like cute cartoon characters (they do rock their tonsures), these two are the Katy Perry and P!nk of the Middle Ages music scene: they know how

16

to PR themselves. As the cathedral is literally built around them and they block out the noise of twelfth-century power tools — chisels and saws — Léonin and Pérotin compose and collect music in Notre Dame and put it into their modestly named *Great Book of Polyphony*. This book will be copied and sent out to the great centres of learning in Europe, because it's not just music and architecture that are expanding …

The population of Europe grows exponentially, more universities are being founded, Fibonacci discovers his sequence, the Magna Carta is signed, reading glasses are invented, manuscripts are commercially copied outside the church, Roger Bacon furthers scientific empiricism ('to ask the proper question is half of knowing'), Thomas Aquinas proposes five ways to prove the existence of God, Genghis Khan invades Hungary. There's not only a huge explosion of knowledge, there's also a huge explosion in ways of seeing the world, especially with your stylish new reading glasses. People are needing more ways to express the growing horizon of their lives, and organum, parallel or not, isn't cutting it in the church service. So composers think, 'Hang on a minute — if we just add a whole new section and new words instead of taking anything away, the church big-wigs won't complain.' And to bind it together they keep the old Gregorian chant as the foundation. It's called the *cantus firmus*, or fixed song, although admittedly the term does make it sound like a back muscle. And that is how we move from plainsong (one voice) to motets (three or more equal voices), often singing completely different words and pitches. Think watching four films at the same time, only much louder.

Music mirrors the changing, often contradictory world of its time. In the 1200s, the mysteries of the world are being discovered, and music is the soundtrack.

Léonin, 'All the Ends of the Earth Have Seen'

Viderunt omnes fines terræ
salutare Dei nostri.
Jubilate Deo, omnis terra.
Notum fecit Dominus salutare suum;
ante conspectum gentium
revelavit justitiam suam.

All the ends of the earth have seen
the salvation of our God.
Rejoice in the Lord, all lands.
The Lord has made known his salvation;
in the sight of the heathen
he has revealed his righteousness.

A single voice breaks the silence, gliding a semitone up to a longer note where the voice is joined by another, perfectly matched on the same pitch. And then a magical event, a splitting of the musical atom, as one voice moves on and the other stays. It is a moment in music history that will not be matched in importance until Arnold Schoenberg and his twelve-tone technique in the twentieth century. From this moment we now hear a direct line to J.S. Bach and his counterpoint, on through to the distinct layers of hip-hop and the dubstep of

Flux Pavilion's 'I Can't Stop'. Now we have a united rhythm and simple harmony.

The united rhythm is achieved with a new way of writing notes: until now, notes had individual heads and tails, or stems. Now the stems are joined into little groups by lines called ligatures. A technique called *melisma*, where one sung syllable can move around on many notes, makes the text less important. So unimportant, in fact, that in this piece, the first thirty-two seconds are taken up by just one syllable — *viiiiiiiiiiiiiiiiiiiiiii iiiiiiiiiiiiiiiiiiiiiiiiiiiiiiiiiiiiiiiiiiiiiiiiiiiiiiiiiiiiiiiiiiiiiiiiiiiiiiiiiiiii* — from *viderunt*. After thirty-two seconds, it's easy to forget where you started. As the top voice settles on a note at the end of a phrase, the bottom voice joins this new pitch; one singer walks up and then down a flight of stairs, and their mate joins them on the steps where they rest.

This is companionable, safe music. This is music which gives an auditory representation of space, even when listened to through headphones. Here is a cathedral made not of stones but of song.

4

Does my ars look good in this?

Question: What does music in the 1300s have in common
with André Rieu and Bryan Adams?
Answer: Waltzes and power ballads.

But first, let's have a little look at the 1300s. And the view is truly shocking.

If you thought living in the twenty-first century was a tad challenging, try fourteenth-century Europe. You remember the population growth of the 1200s? A series of excellent harvests means that when harvests fail catastrophically in the early 1300s, there are so many extra people to feed that the famine wipes out about a quarter of the population. To this day, some villages in France have never recovered. And when a certain flea on a certain rat — and no, we're not talking cutey Ratatouille — arrives in Europe, bringing in its suitcase a dinner suit and the Black Death, people are already weakened, and the results are beyond imagining. In some estimates, half the population of Europe dies in just two years.

A few other things to add to this calamity: endless warfare; the Great Schism with not one, not two, but three popes; further separation of science and religion; decreasing moral leadership of the church; and, weirdly important, the invention of mechanical clocks.

But what does all this mean for music?

A lot. Secular music develops alongside sacred music in a whole new style: ars nova. *Nova*, new, and *ars*, style. Yours is rocking btw.

Motets (remember them? The cantus firmus/Gregorian chant often at the bottom of the sound, with higher voices singing different words) in the new style are included in a popular satirical poem about a naughty horse called Fauvel, and suddenly they are all the rage, both horses and ars nova motets. Now we have music where the different voices, singing completely different parts, are more expressive and united than before. And definitely no more hanging around on one note as your mate wanders off.

And this is where André Rieu wanders — no, waltzes — in. You know André, the waltz king? And you can imagine how a waltz sounds? Waltzes have a strong beat of three, and although they won't be played for a few hundred years yet, they are a good way to illustrate this music. Three is all the rage up to the 1300s; the Holy Trinity pretty much sums it up. When you want a music rhythm then three, called a perfect rhythm, is the go-to. Sorry, go-to-to.

Until it isn't.

Jehan des Murs, a big-brain mathematician, astronomer and musician, possibly influenced by the new way of experiencing time with the new-fangled clocks, is the first to change a rhythm of three into ... wait for it, wait for it ... a rhythm of two. Ta-da! And it has changed its name from perfect rhythm to, you guessed it, imperfect rhythm. Along with splitting those notes into smaller and smaller divisions, a new way of writing it all down invented by a guy called Philippe de Vitry, and grouping these rhythms into even lengths of time called bars, this means that for the first time ever, pitch and rhythm are notated so precisely that music can be accurately recreated anywhere. It's the difference between having a recipe with just a vague list of ingredients, and giving individual measurements and instructions. Proud composers now write their names on their works because their music can be taken from village to town to city and be accurately rendered, so their fortune might be made.

And speaking of stability, the structure of song is now settled in three fixed forms (the ballade, rondeau and verelai), each with set numbers of verses and refrains, echoing similar forms from the Arabian peninsula.

It is now time to meet the dude of ars nova, the rock star of the 1300s, Guillaume de Machaut. Guillaume takes all these new musical changes and rocks them. He writes a whole mass (the first individual to do this), and composes hundreds of popular songs, including early power ballads with syncopated rhythm. Bryan Adams has nothing on this guy — de Machaut sings the Dark Ages version of '(Everything I Do) I Do It For You', and he does it in Old French.

So back to the bubonic plague. Society collapses with the weight of fear and death; work, laws of property and respect for the church fall by the wayside, and if you are sensible, since no-one knows what is causing all this death, death, death, you isolate yourself from everyone. Guillaume de Machaut does just this in 1347 and manages to survive the plague, only coming out of his house when he can hear trumpets and bells ringing. Well, wouldn't you? Come out, that is?

Despite de Machaut staying at home with Netflix, his music is everywhere, including that most bizarre of get-togethers, Black Death parties. Talk about fiddling while Rome burns. As half the European population are dying, some people think, 'Stuff this — if I'm going to die, I'm going to die with a bottle of red and a good tune in my head!'

With death all around, why not listen to a power ballad?

Guillaume de Machaut, 'No More Than a Man'

No more than a man could number the stars
When they are seen to shine so clearly,
And the drops of water in rain and the sea,
And the sands that make up its bed,
Or map the stars in the firmament,
Could anyone fathom or imagine
The great desire I have to see you.

From Hildegard of Bingen and her muted, fragile light, and through the early harmony of Léonin and the sun rising a little, now with Guillaume de Machaut and his love ballad we have a bright, early morning sweep of sound. Here is a dappled light, surprising in the notes it illuminates, receding into brief shadow at the ends of phrases.

De Machaut's harmony is capricious, skittish, delightful; a fresh sound for twenty-first century ears. This ballad is as powerful as any sung by Bryan Adams or Celine Dion, yet here we have only three singers and categorically no drum kit. The high voice, the cantus, has a perfect rhythm in threes, and the two lower voices provide a harmonic grounding with simpler rhythms. When you think of grounding you might imagine a smooth, even surface where your four-legged chair won't wobble. This is not that. This is a floor made from pebbles and earth, where only a three-legged stool will be stable as the rise and fall of the lower parts come in unpredictable waves. This is music to wake you up, music you must follow closely in case it runs away from you. But it is also music where the intricacies are so beguiling, you will never tire of running.

5

It's all about the perspective

A lot has happened since we started just four chapters and four and a half thousand years ago, so shall we have a swift recap?

Here goes. Around 2000 BCE the Harappans, the Mesopotamians then the Ancient Greeks forged the idea of seven notes in an octave; the early Christian church took those pitch systems, or modes, and turned them into plainsong; some monks felt skittish one day and started to add a drone, then went really wild with parallel harmony, then they wanted to show off a bit more and added whole new sections to the mass and so the motet started, with different words for each singer. A new style with snappy syncopations was all the rage during the Black Death and, thanks to Guido of Arezzo, music was written down as precisely as your instructions for the babysitter.

And now, in the early 1400s, we have polyphony: lots of voices, any rhythm we want, and some slightly unpredictable harmony. That is about to change, and for this we can thank the Battle of Agincourt.

One of the most famous and surprising victories for the English against the French, the Battle of Agincourt, starring Kenneth Branagh, means that now the English have rulers in France at the Court of Burgundy, and who needs good music more than a bored noble person? Scores of musicians, the most famous of them John Dunstaple, cross the English Channel (presumably in boats) and bring a new sound: the rich, smooth harmonies of thirds and sixths, not just those parallel fifths. It's the difference between bright blocks of colours side by side and shades between them bringing everything together. A calmness descends. Now music sounds full and rich, a complex stew of flavours rather than a solitary taste. A picture paints a thousand words, but a well-formed motet paints a thousand pictures.

John Dunstaple's music influences French composers like Gilles Binchois and Guillaume Dufay at the Court of Burgundy (the wine list must be good), but it's not just the works of musicians like Dunstaple that influence music. The fall of Constantinople means that Byzantine Greek scholars now make their way to Italy, bringing their Ancient Greek books in their carry-ons. Greek teachings about the individual, humanism and the importance of music from people like Plato are all the rage in 1400s Italy, and we now find ourselves well and truly in the Renaissance.

Visual art is the first to take this renewed view and put the concept of individual perspective into art. In the Renaissance, we can now look at a picture and see things from our own standpoint — we make the picture our own. We can clearly see the difference between mediaeval art, with its naïve representations and lack of perspective, and Renaissance art by looking at two versions of the Madonna and Child, one by Duccio di Buoninsegna painted around 1300, the year of Guillaume de Machaut's birth, and one called *The Madonna of Chancellor Rolin*, by Jan van Eyck (mate of Gilles Binchois) painted in 1435.

In the first the viewpoint is flat, the baby Jesus looks more like a tiny ageing adult than a pudgy infant, and the details of the Madonna's face are distilled into an impenetrable innocence. It is an intimate, straightforward depiction in an iconic style.

And in the second, the differences couldn't be starker — you can smell the pudginess of the baby Jesus, Madonna's expression beguiles with its complexity and subtlety, her cloak is sublimely rendered with every pleat, and the setting of the picture, in a room with pillars looking out to a river and the city, means van Eyck can show off his mastery of perspective. In the distance angles change and objects diminish; the view is yours alone.

And by seeing the difference, we want to hear the difference.

This means those rather lengthy and, you've got to admit, slightly dirgeful plainsongs and organum works are now too vague, all a bit out of focus. Even ars nova doesn't quite cut it. Composers begin to meld the individual voices with each other, creating a gorgeous balance of sound and texture. And they make the music fit the words with word-painting in a deeply human arc of song. The perspective is changed. Not only that, music is now respected as a unique piece of art much like a painting, beginning a tradition we maintain to this day.

So from minimalist plainsong in the Renaissance we now celebrate and hear the glories of all experience.

John Dunstaple, 'Come Creator Spirit'

John Dunstaple is a musical mystery man. Hardly anything is known about him — his life is the 1400s version of coming off social media. Maybe he was born in the English town of Dunstable, maybe he wasn't. There's even a question about whether his name is spelled with a 'p' or a 'b'. Dunstaple works for the Duke of Bedford, a younger brother of Henry V and the same man who orders the burning at the stake of Joan of Arc, a horror Dunstaple may have witnessed. He spends a few years in France and may well have been there for the coronation of Henry VI at Notre Dame, and this motet may, or may not, have been performed at the coronation. Lucky audience. Or not.

So there's a lot we don't know about the musician but, since the music is written down (thanks again, Guido of Arezzo), there is a lot we do know about the manuscripts we have.

This motet is for four voices, the cantus firmus in the bottom part. Always good to have a firmus bottom. And now we get to the bit where music meets maths. Dunstaple is a master of a technique called isorhythm, or equal rhythm. This word, along with diatonic, is a good way to impress your mum. In music it means that the rhythm is repeated throughout to bind the sound together. And in this piece, the repeated rhythm comes three times, the second time one-and-a-half-times as fast, the third time twice as fast. It's music as engineering and gives the motet a compelling momentum. It also gives it a perspective. With its mathematical basis, this technique leaps forward to Johann Sebastian Bach and his *Art of Fugue*, Arnold Schoenberg and his twelve-tone technique, and the minimalist music of Terry Riley, Steve Reich and Arvo Pärt.

So Dunstaple the man remains a mystery, and so does much of his music. During the Reformation in England (Brexit 1500s-style) and the violent dissolution and destruction of the monasteries, much of Dunstaple's music is destroyed; it is only because he is such a star in Europe that his music is saved there for posterity. To think of what posterity loses in England is almost unbearable.

6
Renaissance woman

Imagine trying to live your life, be independent, do what you want to do, go where you want to go, say what you want to say, and you are simply not allowed. Because you are the legal property of either your father, your brother, your husband, or the church. This is the case for all women in Europe in the Renaissance. Well, unless you're a queen.

When we hear stories of female composers from the 1400s and 1500s, we must remember that their achievements are made despite so many impediments. And yet we hear these women's work still. How precious.

There's Vittoria Alleotti, an Italian who, for her musical education and probably not the fashion, enters a convent at fourteen, becomes highly skilled at the harpsichord and singing, and changes her name so now no-one is sure whether she is one woman or two. Intriguing.

There's Caterina Assandra, also working within a convent,

not only singing but playing the organ brilliantly and writing motets where you don't need any male voices. Finally.

And Francesca Caccini, just squeezing into the Renaissance and called 'La Cecchina' — you know you're a superstar when you go by a single name. (Here's looking at you, Madonna.) La Cecchina is a megastar soprano and also happens to write the first opera by a female composer, pithily called *The Liberation of Ruggiero from the Island of Alcina*.

But we are getting a little bit ahead of ourselves and moving into the early 1600s, so let's backtrack to a female composer of the 1500s who, if she were here today, would be taking on the world: Maddelena Casulana.

Maddelena, from a modest background, is offered a chance to study music in Florence and becomes a well-known and highly respected composer of her time. She does not enter a convent but finds ways to make money out in the world by working for the nobility (the Medicis always seem to be up for a party) and composing in the newest style of vocal music — madrigals. So far we have discussed motets (lots of voices singing usually sacred and sometimes secular words), but with madrigals we have fewer voices singing secular words and bringing the drama of those words out with the music. It's a musical style that continues to this day — think Beyoncé and 'Halo', Adele and 'Rolling in the Deep', Björk and, well, anything. These songs are audio paintings of endless drama, tiny operas in their own way, and with her books of madrigals, Maddelena is the first female composer to have her work published. Some people reckon she is the first female to have anything published.

So props to Maddelena — she not only creates a career and a voice for herself, but in the preface to one of her madrigal books she also lets her feelings about the status quo be known:

> [I] want to show the world, as much as I can in this profession of music, the vain error of men that they alone possess the gifts of intellect and artistry, and that such gifts are never given to women.

Maddelena Casulana, composer, singer, businesswoman, sticking it to the man. No, sticking it to the men.

Maddelena Casulana, 'My Heart Cannot Die'
My heart cannot die:
I would like to kill it, since that would please you,
But it cannot be pulled out of your breast
Where it has been dwelling for a long time;
And if I killed it, as I wish,
I know that you would die, and I would die too.

Serious stuff. This passionate number is originally published in a collection of madrigals called *The Desire* (talk about a punchy title), with music by various composers. In total Casulana publishes three of her own books of madrigals; this one is in the first and it's pretty much the number-one hit of her career. And just like Joni Mitchell and Alicia Keys and Katie Noonan to come, Maddelena Casulana creates not only a song but a whole world, a world that provides a deeper meaning of the words, because they are conveyed through music.

Even from the first word — *morir*, die — the music sings the pain, the tragedy, the sweetness of death; the lines of song unite at the word 'heart' and provide a poultice of sound. Pulse and harmony are a relentless force throughout, delineating and changing with each word. 'You would die' is sung six times (talk about a death wish), a trudge through rising semitones of resentment and, with the final phrase 'and I would die too', there is a swift release from suffering. In this song, sound is life, and life is fleeting. The entire song lasts less than two minutes.

We have come a very, very long way since the monks in Notre Dame and their austere chant. Now every word is illustrated as clearly as a graphic novel. This is a remarkable sound world, made even more remarkable when you think of the situation in which women are placed at this time in Europe. They have no rights to anything — education, health, property — and are themselves the property of either their father, brother, uncle, husband or the church. So for Casulana to defy these limitations, to not only deny them but to flourish in spite of them, you've got to want to have her round for dinner sometime. Just don't expect her to do the dishes.

7

Guilding the lily

Being a musician, both now and back in the Renaissance, is not exactly an easy occupation. To defend our rights and conditions, musicians have been gathering in unions, or guilds, since the Middle Ages, and it's not surprising considering musicians have historically been considered social outcasts, denied legal rights and made to work in some pretty dodgy circumstances (yes, I'm looking at you, a certain pop-concert organiser).

So just like many other skilled workers such as carpenters, weavers and metalworkers, by the 1500s musicians are fully organised into guilds, whether they are freelancers or employed by local councils. With these guilds comes better pay and conditions, proper training in the apprentice system and a subsequent rise in musical standards, although if musicians are employed by the nobility, they are expected to work in other positions too, often as barbers and domestic servants. Welcome to 1523 or 2023, take your pick — again, some things never change. Ask the barista what instrument they play next time you buy a coffee.

The 1500s unfurl: Michelangelo takes a big block of marble and finds David inside (how did he know he was there?), Shakespeare finds humanity in his writing, Leonardo da Vinci is introduced to someone called Mona Lisa and agrees to paint her portrait, Copernicus declares the sun the centre of our solar system, the Jesuits are founded, and the rules of musical language are gradually being codified. Finally, none of those dirgeful parallel organums (organi? No, organa) are allowed, the different parts in motets are considered equal (although some are more equal than others) and the high points (and notes) of this time are motets by the Flemish composer Josquin des Prez and the Englishman Thomas Tallis, who outdoes the continental Europeans not perhaps in fashion but certainly in singers — his work 'Spem in Alium (Hope in Any Other)' is for forty — yes, forty — individual voices.

There are varying stories of the reason for this work: it may have been composed for the fortieth birthday of Elizabeth I, it may have been composed to outdo an Italian dude who also writes a motet for forty voices, or it may have been written for Mary Tudor. It may have been written for an earl with an octagonal dining hall and balconies. Lucky him. Whatever the reason for the composition, Tallis sensibly splits the ensemble into eight choirs of five singers each. Much easier to herd and be heard.

The music, with that much potential, that much heft, strikes your ears as the sun strikes a distant mountain range. The choirs enter one by one, simultaneously falling and rising, sometimes singing on their own, sometimes all forty voices rising as one to declare the power of God. The beauty of 'Spem in Alium' is perhaps only matched in nature by the wind blowing across a meadow of pliant grass. What must be the effect of this piece in the 1500s, when life is short and so much of that short life is a mystery, when the loudest sound is a thunderstorm or an avalanche, and when music of this type is still very much for the privileged few? This motet leads, in many centuries to come, towards Górecki's *Symphony of Sorrowful Songs* with its perpetuity of solace.

Listen, and weep.

So much music is deeply beautiful in the Renaissance. In fact, you may not want to go any further in music and just rest here for a while, admiring the view. Many musicians do just that and make their careers out of playing this music alone. (These musicians obviously are not allowed to use electricity and must go to their gigs on horseback, or a horse and cart if they play the viola da gamba.)

Renaissance composers take the Ancient Greek ideals of using different orders of notes, or modes, for different emotions, and with them accentuate the poetry of song, which is now in your own language rather than Latin. This really is heaven on a stick.

And then along comes Gesualdo.

Who?

Gesualdo. Carlo Gesualdo, Prince of Venosa to you. Gesualdo could be described by talking about him stabbing his wife and her lover to death when he discovers them *in flagrante delicto*, or him paying men night after night to beat him up in a BDSM kind of way, or his tragic periods of profound depression. Or Gesualdo might be described by listening to his music.

Because this stuff is wild. Gesualdo uses not just the regular notes of the modes, the so-called *musica recta* or straight music, the notes we have been listening to all this time; he packs his madrigals with *musica ficta*, false music, all the notes in between or what we now call the chromatic notes. Kind of like fake news but ... not. Chromatic means colourful, so if you think of the regular notes being the primary and secondary colours, we are now moving into tertiary colour territory. Maybe even with some fluorescents thrown in. That's why you might have trouble whistling along to Gesualdo's music. He not only turns those sweet, harmonious developing sounds of the 1500s on their handsome little heads, his musical style is not repeated until easily the middle twentieth century by atonal composers like Alban Berg and Anton Webern. Finding Gesualdo's music in the 1500s is as bizarre as seeing a solar-powered drone in the sky or hearing a hip-hop song down ye olde musicke shoppe. With Gesualdo, we realise that music will come in its own time, and all we can do is listen.

Carlo Gesualdo, 'Moro, lasso, al mio duolo (I Die, Alas, in My Suffering)'

We were talking in the last chapter about women in the 1500s having no rights, and that appears to also apply to the right to life itself. When Gesualdo murders his wife, Maria d'Avalos, he is not prosecuted for it because it is a nobleman's right to kill his wife. So when Gesualdo wants to get married again, he is completely free to do so, and amazingly, he finds a brave noblewoman, Eleanora d'Este from Ferrara, to marry him (although her family does draw up a contract). The marriage goes horribly wrong horribly quickly — Eleanora ends up suing Gesualdo's mistress, who is tried and found guilty of witchcraft with another woman and both are sentenced to live in Gesualdo's castle. Hmm, not quite sure what the punishment is there. Anyhoo, marrying a noblewoman from Ferrara is quite the career move for Gesualdo, as Ferrara is a major music centre and has one of the newly emerging choirs of professional female singers, or *concerto della donne*. Up to now, madrigals have been fairly easy to sing, but with the rise of professional choirs and their increased skill, madrigals become more and more virtuosic. The combination of this vocal ability and Gesualdo's unstable state of mind means that his music is unpredictable, to say the least.

Harmony, with its progression from one chord to the next, is a pathway through music. Up to now we have had a simple, straight path. The path becomes more bendy with the new Renaissance harmonies, but still there is a clear way ahead; we can predict where we are going. With Gesualdo's harmony, especially in 'Moro, lasso', the path veers wildly off to the left or right, turns back on itself, is patchy and overgrown or sometimes simply disappears altogether. Harmonic doors slink and slide, opening and closing on a parallel universe of sound. We slope from one world into another, the sky now green, the grass blue, and we slip again to a planet of impenetrable air and floating water. In this madrigal of Gesualdo's, we can predict absolutely nothing. The harmonic path is on fire — no, it's collapsed into a sinkhole. Gesualdo is a murderer, a misogynist, a masochist; he also creates music that foreshadows the psychological explorations of Freud and Jung three hundred years hence.

With 'Moro, lasso', Gesualdo makes music as dangerous as he is himself.

8

Music means business

It's 1501 and you've just come back from town (where you've managed to avoid someone chucking their cooking water all over your nice new ruff) with some sheet music made using the very latest technology. You can hardly believe the reasonable price and clarity of the printing of this volume of songs from Italy. In your hands you hold music printed for the first time with moveable type. No more manuscripts on dried animal skins, no more waiting ages for someone to copy the music note by note, no more dodgy woodblock printing where you need to squint and hope the choirmaster doesn't notice when you stuff up.

And beyond all that, these songs look gorgeous: Petrucci, the Venetian printer, has put the paper through the press three times: first for the lines or stave, next for the words, and third for the notes. Music isn't going to look this good again until ... well, music will never look this good again. (Btw, you can see this music the next time you visit New York's public library.) Moveable-type music printing is the biggest breakthrough since Guido of

Arezzo's notation way back in the eleventh century, and it means that music is now cheaper and more widely available, especially outside the church, new songs are disseminated more quickly, and those national styles really take root. Because now not only the church and the nobility have music books, nearly everyone does.

Music is no longer a service — music is now a business.

In England, Queen Elizabeth I grants William Byrd and Thomas Tallis (he of forty-voices, 'Spem in Alium' fame) a monopoly of music printing. Not just printing music, but even printing the five-line stave and nothing else. You would think this is a tasty deal, but not even a great deal can make up for poor business practice. These two should stick to composing, as after a few years in the music-publishing trade, they need to ask the queen for some land to make up for their losses. Whoops. Maybe they should get into bitcoin.

Those losses *are* surprising because business is booming. From the beginning of the Renaissance, the study of music is central to a good education, and as trade spreads throughout Europe and beyond, the middle classes grow; they are well-educated and they *really* want to play music. Sure, you can become a professional musician and learn mostly in the aural tradition, but how much handier to be able to sit down with your mates, have a few drinks and read through the latest madrigal music from Florence. And this way you don't have to be a barber *and* a gamba player.

The music-loving and -buying public really is born in this time, and you might say that nothing will change so radically for music until the invention of recording.

The church has always recognised the power of music, even more so now as learning music is accessible to so many. Do you remember the Council of Laodicea? You may have put it out of your head because it's so damn shocking, but quick recap: about 1200 years ago by now, the head church guys decided that the congregation shouldn't sing in church, only the dudes up at the ambo. Well, that is about to change, and frankly, it's about time after a thousand years.

You may want to stand back a little, as here comes a man who will completely transform the sound and making of music within the church. His name is Martin Luther. You may have heard of him. He is holding a hammer and with that sturdy hammer he is about to nail his ninety-five theses to the church door in Wittenberg.

Bang. Bang. BANG.

One of the tenets of Luther's reformation is about music. He believes that music is a gift from God, and that God's message can be better transmitted through song. It can also be better transmitted when the words are in German, not Latin. And Luther doesn't want just the guys at the front singing — he wants everyone to join in. Finally. Luther not only wants the whole world to sing, he also has a good ear for a tune, writing his own music and taking popular songs from the street and bringing them into the church in the form of harmonised songs, or chorales. These are some of the first mashups in music. Luther is not only a religious pioneer but also a musical one, and we hear his influence all the way through Johann Sebastian Bach to Fanny and Felix Mendelssohn, Johannes Brahms, Anton

Bruckner, Sofia Gubaidulina and Elena Kats-Chernin. Martin Luther brings music back to the people.

As the Reformation surges, and then the Counter-Reformation, with Catholic composers like Orlando di Lasso, Tomàs Luis de Victoria and Giovanni Pierluigi da Palestrina lifting their game, music reaches glories and sounds simply unimaginable even a century earlier. Music is greater than us all.

Giovanni Pierluigi da Palestrina, 'The Sorrowful Mother Standing'

Palestrina is born just outside of Rome in, you guessed it, Palestrina, and spends most of his life as a choirmaster in various churches, including St Peter's Basilica in the Vatican. Before Palestrina comes along, the leading composers of this time are Josquin des Prez and the Northern Europeans. Palestrina changes everything.

You remember those plainsong Gregorian chants dictated from a dove? Clean-lined, pure and plain? Palestrina takes these chants, reaching an ear, a hand back a thousand years, and now they are transformed — the holes are fixed, there's a new bathroom, the ceilings have been painted and they are almost unrecognisable. This is one of the greatest remodelling jobs in history. Luther might use popular tunes of the decade, but Palestrina uses popular tunes of the millennium.

With the 'Stabat Mater', his setting of the twelfth-century text, Palestrina opens our eyes wide to the possibilities of harmony. His music moves serenely through chords and over dissonances as if they are hardly there, mere blips in the chord progression of life. Palestrina's ear is not on the world as it is — his ear is on the world as it could be.

9

Where are all the instruments?

So up to now you've heard a lot of music, but it's been mostly vocal. Well, apart from the most popular sound of the 4500s BCE, the gishgudi. And you may be thinking that outside of pub music, where are all the instruments? Good question.

It's all to do with the church. You will have noticed that much of the music we have heard so far was written in or for or by the Christian church, and they only had vocal music, hence the phrase for 'a choir alone,' *a cappella*, meaning in the style of the chapel. But now, in the sixteenth century, the middle classes are expanding and they want to play more music. They don't only want to — they are expected to. A person without music in their life is considered suspicious and of poor character; it must be true because Shakespeare says so in *The Merchant of Venice*. Doing a bit of paraphrasing, a person who doesn't have music in their life is dull, traitorous, mean and untrustworthy. And who wants to be that? Society expects people of a certain class, and who want to stay in that certain class, to play music with just the right amount of skill: not too much, not too little. This is especially true for women, who are expected to learn music so they can attract a high-quality husband. Now that you can buy sheet music in most towns because it is easily and inexpensively printed, playing instrumental music at home comes into fashion.

And there is nothing more fashionable than the lute. A perfect match with your ruff, buckled shoes and two-tone hosiery, the lute is descended from the Arabic oud and is the go-to instrument for solo playing and singer-songwriter coolness. A sixteenth-century version of the electric guitar.

If you want something with a fuller sound you could try the hurdy-gurdy, where the strings are sounded by a wheel turned by a handle (it does sound like something from Bunnings) and the notes are changed with wooden keys. A sort of piano meets hand drill situation. If you'd like something more sensual or you'd just like an excuse to sit down, how about the new viola da gamba, or viola of the leg? As you need to sit with your legs a little open, the viola da gamba is considered unsuitable for ladies. There will be a viola of the arm as well, the viola da braccio, but we will just have to wait a bit. The viola da gamba has developed from the Arabian rebab and the guitar-like vihuela; just like Jimmy Page in years to come, some cool person decided they didn't want to pluck it anymore and bowed it instead. With that the family of viola da gambas is born and, a little later, something called the violin, smaller and louder than the viola da gamba and usually played for dancing. Crucially, you can play it standing up and have a dance yourself.

For keyboard instruments, you could have a go at the harpsichord or, for something quieter, the clavichord, both of which are developed from the virginals, or double virginals (this is sounding stranger and stranger) if it has two keyboards. The virginals, for some reason always spoken about in the plural, is so named because it is played by young women. And don't forget the organ: there is a portable or portative organ, and a positive (in position) organ. You could try the negative organ but there isn't one.

And for wind instruments, why not have a go on the crumhorn (an early oboe), the sackbut (a proto-trombone) or the recorder, an early recorder? Consorts, or ensembles, of either loud or soft instruments were formed in the Middle Ages and played depending on whether you wanted to have a nap or not, and in the Renaissance they continue, gradually mixing more varied instruments. As a musician you would be expected to play the whole of your family of instruments (it would be like learning the violin, viola, cello and double bass — you'll need a really, *really* big horse and cart to get to gigs), so completely different from nowadays where most people learn a single instrument. We have the French to thank for that — more when we reach the French Revolution in two hundred years and about sixty pages' time.

The music you play in these years could be arrangements of vocal music, gazillions of dances, variations on popular songs or, thanks to musicians doodling a bit on their instruments, something more abstract: chaconnes from South America and Spain, preludes, fantasias, toccatas, symphonies and early sonatas, meaning literally 'sounded', originally an addition to the mass. This is a seismic shift for music: here is music purely for its own sake and sound without relying on a story or words. This is the moment Johannes Brahms will come back to when he is fighting with Richard Wagner in a few centuries. Now pieces are written for specific players and spaces — Giovanni Gabrieli's music, for example, is composed specially for the enormous space of St Mark's Basilica in Venice.

So you get the feeling that most of the music we hear now very much has its roots in the sixteenth century, in its form, content, name and intent. You could even say the sixteenth century is when modern music started.

Giovanni Gabrieli, Sacred Symphonies

St Mark's Basilica in Venice. Here is a structure originally built to house the relics of St Mark, whose body was smuggled out of Egypt by hiding it under layers of pork fat. The original building burned down and the current one is bestowed ('decorated' doesn't seem quite significant enough) with four bronze horses from the Fourth Crusade. Even before entering this place, you can feel the force is strong here.

If you are used to the cold, bare stone of northern European cathedrals, when you enter St Mark's your visual senses are blasted with golden cannon, because virtually all the walls and ceiling are covered in gold. Not just a bit of flaky gold paint here and there — this is making-a-statement gold, with gold mosaic iconography of Christ and his disciples that somehow makes the gold even ... golder.

As your eyes are given a vitamin A shot of colour, your ears are tuned into the sounds. Because here is Giovanni Gabrieli standing to one side of the basilica and directing his instrumentalists in one of his Sacred Symphonies. Gabrieli would not think very much of today's sound systems because he has the best sound system in the world: the space of St Mark's Basilica in Venice. He has not spent any of his composing time on dances — nothing so frivolous for him. His music is all about the church and worshipping God as fully and with the richest and most satisfying sound as possible. Here is balance, contrast, division and unison in a single arc of music.

A choir of brass players is positioned around the basilica in the opposing choir lofts to create a double wall of sound. Gabrieli understands the drama, the majesty, the sheer bloody thrill of loud music, and when these trumpets, cornets (like a recorder but with a brass mouthpiece) and sackbuts really get going, there is nothing more glorious, more visceral, more stimulating. His music dances, swirls, throbs, inspires and reduces us to tiny specks in his planet of noise.

Who needs words when you are surrounded by sackbuts?

10

All change for the 1600s!

If you will, cast your mind back to the 1300s. Remember the devastation wreaked by famine and plague, and how that influenced the music of its time? Rhythm became more playful, with syncopation and faster notes, and people turned to music because death, death, death was *everywhere*.

Now fast-forward to the 1600s and, tragically, we are back in that same place. The Little Ice Age diminishes crop production, and widespread war diminishes the population — by up to fifty percent in some places. And yet, despite the 1600s being ravaged by violence, it is an age of scientific and cultural glories in every facet.

The scientific revolution reveals that planets go around the sun — we can now observe them with our new telescopes — and Sir Isaac Newton shows how much can be revealed with the application of calculus. (If you're feeling a little troubled by school memories at the use of the word 'calculus', apologies. Go watch some Eddie Woo videos later.)

Economies turn towards a system where people give their money to businesses, who in turn give them some of it back if they make a profit. It's called capitalism … you may have heard of it. This leads to stock companies combining the wealth of many and taking financial power to more of the people, not just the monarchy, aristocracy and the church.

In literature, the 1600s fill your bookshelves with those writers you like to have behind you on Zoom calls — Molière, Racine, Ben Jonson, John Donne, Milton and Cervantes — and architecture and painting fill your view with complexity, decoration and sensuality. Think the Schönbrunn Palace in Vienna, the Cathedral of Santiago de Compostela in Barcelona, St Peter's Square in Rome. The polar opposites of minimalist.

It's a brave new world, the 1600s, and people need an outer description of their inner existence. Western music has grown with the significant contributions of inventions outside of Europe — the seven-note system from Mesopotamia, paper and printing from China, the lute from Egypt, viols from Mongolia — and now, to continue that growth, the first public subscription concerts are organised. Once again power, this time in music, is given to the people. As a parallel to combining wealth through capitalism, the first orchestras are founded combining the skills of different players. With scientific breakthroughs and new analysis of affections by people like Descartes (you are thinking of doughnuts therefore you are a doughnut), composers are taking an analytic approach to the different emotions. Different keys are aligned with different emotions — D major equals triumph, A-flat minor a wailing lament — and there is a move away from Ancient Greek modes to an establishment of major and minor tonality. This is the time when abstract music really roots itself, with new inventions like the chaconne, trio sonata, overture, concerto, suite and fugue. Claudio Monteverdi takes the madrigal and makes it a perfect world; the art of polyphony, with many different voices, is refined more and more with counterpoint, organising those many voices so they make musical sense and a coherent whole. Think a chorus versus a crowd. No longer and never more will music only be tied to religious words. Now music is tied to life itself.

And the new name for this bold, elaborate new style? Well, it's a word that originally means bizarre, in bad taste, or misshapen. We are now firmly in the baroque, and there isn't a bad taste around.

Girolamo Frescobaldi, First Book of Canzons

Frescobaldi isn't a composer frequently on people's top-twenty list of composers. He might not even make the top hundred, and that's a shame, because Frescobaldi has some of the freshest sounds around in the early baroque period. And maybe, after you listen to some of these songs (which a canzon is just a fancy name for), you'll put him in your top ten. You'll be in good company — J.S. Bach himself is a big fan.

You remember Palestrina and Gesualdo? Okay, things are starting to slot into place — Frescobaldi works at St Peter's in the Vatican, the same basilica as Palestrina but just a few years later, and Frescobaldi comes from the town of Ferrara, which is where Gesualdo (wild harmonies and wife murderer) moves to improve his career and find another unsuspecting wife. Monteverdi also turns up in Ferrara and has extended chats with Frescobaldi about music styles. Sort of Facebook Live rather than Snapchat. It's a small pond, the music world, and easy to play the Kevin Bacon game.

Frescobaldi is the first composer to dedicate himself to plumbing the depths of instrumental music (and with the sackbut, that really is plumbing). He is also one of the first composers to make secular music as prominent in his output as sacred music, thanks to wealthy patrons like the Medici family, and various cardinals who like a spot of secular dancing on a Friday night in their red tap shoes. Frescobaldi is also one of the first musicians to use a wide variety of speeds, or tempi — think 'Bohemian Rhapsody' plus oddly similar haircuts. This man, who may be rapidly making his way up your list, also composes pieces on top of pieces — a palimpsest of music. When you combine that with his changes in speed, you have a serious contender for Best Trance Music Award 1628.

This music, mostly for a selection of instruments plus bass and harpsichord, is a book of songs for Frescobaldi's mates. A sort of musical social diary, dedicating each of the pieces to a different friend or patron. The different pieces are a mixed tape of emotions; sometimes gleeful and rapid, sometimes morose and melancholic. Poetic, you might say, although friends of Frescobaldi say he doesn't understand poetry and needs to ask his wife to explain it to him. With this music, itself sonic poetry, you must wonder whether those friends are more like frenemies.

11

Prima donnas and divas

You're in luck. It's October 1600 and you're holding an invitation to *the* social event of the year, the marriage of Maria de' Medici and King Henri IV of France. It's going to be beyond glamorous, and besides the fashion, the intrigue and the food, the entertainment is looking pretty special. First up, there's a horse ballet (known for their pliés) and in the evening there's something called an opera.

A what?

An opera. From the Italian word for work, and the text is called a *libretto*, little book. It's a whole new art form for the European folks of 1600. Not for Chinese people though — opera has been performed in China since 200 CE.

As you now know, by the 1600s singing has been central to Western music-making for over a thousand years. Whether it's praising God down the church or praising hedonism down the pub, masses and motets and madrigals and ballades all have the human voice at their heart. And as you also know, Ancient

Greek beliefs in the noteworthiness (pardon the pun) of music are upheld by many.

Around the turn of the century, two important things are discovered:

1. the chorus in Greek plays would have been sung, and
2. a guy called Girolamo Mei discovers that Greek music pretty much always consisted of a single melody.

Hang on a minute. Hasn't music just spent the last several hundred years getting away from a single melody? Didn't those monks get bored and start to add new words and lines and we ended up with polyphony? Exactly. And that's not going away just yet, but Girolamo chats with a group of scholars, the Florentine Camerata, and recommends the very old way of doing things. The idea is picked up by Galileo Galilei's dad, Vincenzo, and he brings us back to the old, very old, way of music — monody, or accompanied solo singing. And with that stamp of approval from some of the most powerful thinkers of their time, composers experiment with a new form called an aria. These arias, combined with another art form called intermedio, where complex instrumental and vocal music is played between acts of a play, finally come together in the first ever European opera, *Dafne* by Jacopo Peri. And it's a classic opera story: Greek god Apollo becomes obsessed with nymph Dafne; Dafne saves herself by transforming into a laurel tree. Unfortunately, somebody isn't very careful with the sheet music (maybe it's also turned into a laurel tree) because most of it is now lost; the first performance at a late-night carnival may have something to do with it. There's bound to be a few beer stains.

Back to the wedding with the dancing horses. Peri gets the gig of his life when his opera *L'Euridice* is performed there, but wait, he gives us more. The shock of the new is not just that a story can now be told with music throughout — what Peri also does is invent a way of singing that rings through to this day with its particular style of rhythmic speech mixed with song. It's called recitative style, and we hear it in rap, hip-hop, sprechstimme and, yes, Rex Harrison.

So before long, many composers have jumped on the opera train. Well, opera cart. Francesca Caccini is the first female to compose an opera, a comedy called *The Liberation of Ruggiero*, and Monteverdi is the composer who brings opera to early glories, especially with his *Coronation of Poppea*. Barbara Strozzi, singer and composer, never writes an actual opera but does write a lot of cantatas and arias comprising devastatingly tragic music to go with her favourite theme — unrequited love.

But the last word should perhaps be given to a new genre of star, the diva and the divo. As high-budget shows are made or broken by show-stopping arias, the people delivering those arias, the singers, become the most important on the stage (or under it, or behind it), and their name describes their VIP status: the *prima donna* or *primo uomo*, first woman or first man. And in a rare situation for this time, being a woman is a tad more appealing than being a bloke, as the boys are castrated to maintain their high voices. Ouch.

Claudio Monteverdi, 'I Gaze upon You', *The Coronation of Poppea*

Here is a fence, low and open, loosely dividing the end of the Renaissance and the beginning of the baroque, and over there is a handsome guy, straddling it in his boots and lace collar. His name is Claudio Monteverdi and this bloke is the poster boy of the early 1600s with his biker-boy moustache and goatee. Monteverdi composes a gazillion madrigals in complex polyphony and elegant counterpoint, then knocks out a bunch of operas with some of the best tunes ever. Here's one of those tunes, 'Pur ti miro' — I gaze upon you, I desire you, I embrace you, I enchain you.

Oh dear. It was all going so well until that last phrase.

Things are not always easy for Monteverdi. His madrigal style can be too jittery for some (he has a bit of a Gesualdo thing going on), and he is passed over for a big gig when he's apparently at the height of his career in his thirties. His music is attacked in a pamphlet (the Twitter of the 1600s) for being too emotional, but this only makes Monteverdi

a) carry on composing the same way, and
b) even more famous.

But what Monteverdi does do, alongside his jittery music, is continue the polyphonic style of Palestrina and that very 'churchy' sound, making sure the glories of the Counter-Reformation sing on into the 1700s and beyond. He codifies emotions into love, war and calmness, with musical styles to match, and predates musique concrète by four hundred years with his use of distinctly unmusical sounds. Monteverdi becomes the music director of St Mark's in Venice, taking over the gig from Gabrieli, and when he is more than seventy years old and the first public opera houses open in Venice, his career takes on a whole new lease of life. *Now* he is at the height of his career. Monteverdi really is the Duracell Bunny of music.

This aria from his last opera, *The Coronation of Poppea*, is full of the complexities and slants of love. Monteverdi has such a sense for melody, 'Pur ti miro' is one of the first tunes in this little history you might want to sing at karaoke. Here is a duet between the lovers, beginning as an echo and becoming the warp and weft of beauty. Monteverdi — who at this point in his life has worked all over Italy, met some of the greatest people of his age, been both turned down for jobs and given enormous responsibility, lost his wife and survived the bubonic plague — distils all his knowledge of life's ache and acme into one simple tune. It is futile, it is perfect.

Next time you're at the St Mary of the Friars Church in Venice, just next to the Leonardo da Vinci Museum, say hello to Monteverdi. And if no-one's around, maybe you can sing a little of 'Pur ti miro' to him to say thank you, and to tell him that his music is not forgotten.

12

Musical codes and twirly bits

Hello again —welcome back to the 1600s!

Last time we chatted you might not have been able to hear that well as there was a lot of this (INSERT LOUD OPERA SINGING) and a surprising number of these (INSERT NEIGHS). We were talking about polyphony — lots of musical lines at once — and reverting to the Ancient Greek way of doing things, monody, one line with an accompaniment. Think Ed Sheeran with his little guitar. Hang on a minute ... Is Ed Sheeran just really tall?

Around this time, composers are writing music for singers, but with a special part for the organ to play just the lowest notes of the piece. This is for when there aren't enough singers (they're at their day job) and the organ needs to fill in a bit, since we listeners are now used to and expect gorgeous harmonies.

There's a problem, though. The organ part only has single bass notes, no chords. So the organists need to guess what other notes to play and they keep getting it wrong. Badly.

So please welcome, organ left, a dude called Agostino Agazzari. Just like Guido of Arezzo, the guy who brought us the five-line stave, Agazzari feels the pain (and hears the wrong notes) of the organists and vows to make a code, a code so simple that they know which notes to play on top of the bass notes. The code is called figured bass (go figure), and it is literally playing by numbers.

Agazzari prints numbers below the bass notes — if there's a 4 and a 6 written under a C, the keyboard player plays the C and the notes four and six above it. Easy.

Or not.

Because as a keyboard player, you don't just play straight chords. You must also add a counter melody, or counterpoint, into your part, all improvised, made up completely on the spot. When you consider you do this on the fly and with the correct rhythm, style and emotion, oh and looking good for whichever duchess you're playing for, all with a castrato singer belting a tune out in your ear, there is, frankly, a lot going on. And you need to keep playing continuously, hence the new name, basso continuo. As the basso continuo develops and other instruments are added — theorbo (that's the lute that looks like a giraffe and you don't take on the bus), a bassoon (*Rumpole of the Bailey*) or a viola da gamba (you'd better find them a nice chair) — you might be starting to realise this basso continuo gig is a tough one. And that it's somehow familiar. Hang on a minute: a bass, some rhythm, some chords ... Oh yes. Your quintessential rock band. Figured bass + grunge cardigan = Nirvana.

And you might also be thinking, well, if the composer is just adding a few bass notes and numbers, but the bass continuo players are adding all the colour, aren't they kind of like co-composers, you know, a sort of Lennon/McCartney vibe? That's true, although they don't get a credit and certainly not any royalties. But it gets better. In the 1600s, composers also expect performers to add decorations to the music, extra and often very fast notes to literally decorate the basic music. It's the difference between a simple Shaker chair and the magnificent and terrifying swordy seat of power in *Game of Thrones* — they are both essentially chairs, but one has people napping in it and the other has inspired a lot of war and bloodshed. These extra notes draw the sparkle and energy out of an otherwise ordinary tune. For instance, if the composer has written one long note, the performer is expected to decorate the note with a repeated sound above it, like a bird's trill (it's called a trill) or do a little turn around the note (it's called a turn). There, music theory. So easy. The skill lies in not doing too much or too little. The performers will develop this skill through years of practice, but the belief is they play the extra notes through inspiration or the grace of God, hence the extra notes become known as, you guessed it, grace notes.

We hear them throughout music and time, from seventeenth-century baroque sonatas through Frederick Chopin and his elegant brush of sound, to Ella Fitzgerald with her dance around a song, and Billie Eilish with her intricate web in melody.

Grace and figured bass. The baroque period has something for everyone.

François Couperin, Pieces for Viola da Gamba with Figured Bass

François Couperin, a French composer and keyboard player who works for the Sun King, Louis XIV, is one of those guys for whom things just seem to work out. Well, apart from losing his dad at a very young age. People make their own luck, you could say, and Couperin is a hard worker — he takes on his dad's position as organist at a Paris church when he is about eleven, wins the gig to work for the king and then asks the king for his royal assent to publish music. You remember William Byrd and Thomas Tallis in the 1500s, asking Queen Elizabeth I for some land to make up for their music publishing losses even though they have the monopoly in the whole country? Those guys were bad businessmen. Couperin is not. He publishes a 'harpsichord for dummies' manual, a bunch of music for small, or chamber, groups and, just before he dies at the not-so-ripe age of sixty-three composes these pieces for viola da gamba and figured bass. If you ever need a reason to learn the viola da gamba, this might be it. All you need to do now is find one.

The true beauty of these pieces lies in the skill of the performer interpreting Couperin's subtle markings for grace notes. Even from the very beginning, Couperin adds little signs to show there should be a little slide of notes here, another two or three there, all left to the performer to interpret and feel the mood, the groove, the vibe of the piece. It will change from concert to concert, hall to hall, day to day, according to the mood of the performer, and even what they have for breakfast. And what could be more delicious than a continental breakfast?

13

Eurovision, 1600s-style

It's May in Europe and you know what that means. No, not the end of the English Civil War no, not the famine in France that kills two million no, not the Franco-Dutch War; and no, not Sir Isaac Newton playing with apples. It's May, so it's Eurovision, 1600s-style!

Sure, the English might have some good tunes and a refreshing take on music after their civil war, and okay, the Italians are always going to have the best clothes, shoes and fancy beats, and you're right, the Spanish music theatre, the zarzuela, is tops for drama, but year after year, it's the French who are taking all the prizes. And that's because someone called Louis has realised that whoever controls music controls minds. That someone you might know better as Louis XIV, aka the Sun King (no relation to the Lion King, although the music's as good).

This Louis is crucial for France's success in late 1600s Eurovision for a few reasons.

First, he is king for a long time, seventy-two years in fact, so his ideas have an opportunity to bed in, you might say. He is what we call an absolute monarch, and to hold onto absolute power he projects a propaganda image of himself aligned with Apollo, the Greek sun god, hence the Sun King. He ensures absolute control over all the arts and sciences by establishing centralised academies, and he establishes the Palace of Versailles, where he gathers all the French nobility and rarely lets them leave. Think *Dangerous Liaisons* and a large and fancy prison.

Tidy work if you're a monarch, but also tricky as you now have a lot of bored aristocracy needing to be entertained. To control the entertainment, Louis invites the very best French musicians to work for him, among them Marin Marais, star viola da gamba player, and Élisabeth Jacquet de La Guerre, a harpsichordist who works for one of the Sun King's extramarital girlfriends. Louis goes on to create three divisions of musicians for his (and the nobility's) pleasure: the Chapel, the Chamber and the Stables.

The Chapel are performers for religious music, mostly singers; the Chamber for sexy chamber music (that would be the string instruments); and the Stable musicians are the party animals, sorry, louder ones — brass, drums, winds. This specialisation (and a stable Stable job) means there is time and money to improve instruments in both make and technique — the shawm, a descendant of the dreaded aulos, inspires a whole new instrument, the oboe, and the horn is developed with new metal alloys into a loop. Now it can be foisted over a player's shoulder and off they go on their horse, the bell of the horn blowing out over the horse's bottom and signalling to the riders behind, who are now going a bit deaf. As the French are so important to the dawn of the horn, the instrument is sometimes called a French horn, but just don't call it that to a horn player. It's a HORN. Sometimes, if the musicians from the three divisions have been well-behaved and the king wants a big celebration, they play all together, thus creating the first orchestras.

French music, more elegant and refined than any other, really shines in two ways: ballet and opera. In both there is one composer who dances and sings above them all — Jean-Baptiste Lully.

Lully's career begins as a dancer and an Italian teacher, but he must have more than some pretty calf muscles and fancy verb declinations, as the Sun King quickly makes him head of the royal violin ensemble and superintendent of the royal music. Those orchestras that are just starting up around this time must be rowdy places to work, because to keep control of the musicians, in a music version of absolute power, Lully institutes a dictatorial way of conducting that is copied by a fair few conductors down the years (here's looking at you, Herbert von Karajan). And instead of a tiny baton you can hold with two fingers, in the 1600s the conductor uses a stout cane, like a walking stick, which they bang on the floor beside them to keep the beat.

That bossiness is the thing that does Lully in, though: he bangs his conducting cane so hard that he stabs himself in the foot and dies of gangrene. Once again, ouch.

Jean-Baptiste Lully, *The Bourgeois Gentleman*

Autumn 1670. Here we are in the Loire Valley at the Château de Chambord, hunting lodge for the king of France. After a day's hunting, what better than to put your feet up and watch a new play by Molière: *The Bourgeois Gentleman*, a play with dancing and music, and the hit of the year. And here comes Lully, dressed in full laciness and fluffiness, curly concert wig on his head, conducting cane topped with gold in his hand, stepping up to take charge of this new-fangled orchestra. Lully has had a meteoric rise to fame after coming from Florence, teaching Italian and dance to French nobility, and now in charge of all the king's music and admired throughout Europe. Not bad for the son of a miller. Lully bangs his cane, the overture begins, and now you can hear why the French always win Eurovision in the 1600s. The rhythms dance and provoke, the variety of instruments means you are never bored with the sound, and all the time Lully is there with his cane, frowning at the musicians, exhorting them to greater unity, elegance and virtuosity of grace notes. This surely is reason enough to believe the Sun King has divine inspiration. There is no other sound like this, the orchestra from Versailles in all their sartorial and musical finery. This is music fit for a Dancing Queen.

14

Those mean, mean tones

Ice cream, telescopes, banknotes, calculus, dictionaries, calculators. The 1600s in Europe have been so full of discoveries that this time is dubbed the Scientific Revolution, but this logical way of thinking is not restricted to science.

You remember a couple of chapters ago we talked about Vincenzo Galilei, Galileo's dad and the guy who suggested going back to solo melody and accompaniment? What you're about to hear may blow your mind, but he also suggests we have twelve notes in an octave instead of seven. Talk about earth-shattering. It's not long after Vincenzo's proposal that bewigged and bejewelled composer Jean-Philippe Rameau writes one of the most important works *ever* in the history of Western music, his *Treatise on Harmony*. Available now at all good bookshops. Realistically, you might have to order it in.

The title page of Rameau's treatise is surprisingly moving, perhaps because of the simplicity of his language, or perhaps it's the aspiration of the subject matter:

TREATISE ON HARMONY
Reduced to its natural principles
Divided into four books
Book I: On the relationship between
harmonic ratios and proportions.
Book II: On the nature and properties of chords; and on
everything which may be used to make music perfect.
Book III: Principles of composition.
Book IV: Principles of accompaniment.
By MONSIEUR RAMEAU
Organist of the Cathedral of Clermont in Auvergne

With this treatise, Rameau brings together all the ideas about harmony that have been developing organically over the last few centuries. He takes the notes of the harmonic series, with the octaves, thirds and fifths as the most important, and organises a logical system where these primary notes played together make triads using the first, third and fifth notes of a scale — the building blocks of our harmony to this day. It is triads that make up the chords you play on your guitar in your garage band, it is triads that make the blues blue and make you laugh or cry. It is triads that change the way we hear the world. With this system we move from Ancient Greek and church modes to major and minor tonality and the world of keys — C minor, E-flat major and so on. It is also the codified moment when we move from a horizontal, melodic way of thinking, as in Indian classical music, to a vertical, harmonic way of thinking. You're getting the idea. This is a *massive* moment.

You may want to have a slice of cake and just ruminate for a while.

In a neat parallel with another part of nature, the notes of the basic triad align with the primary colours: red, yellow and blue are the first, third and fifth colours in the rainbow.

By now you may have noticed how codified Western music is becoming, with notation, harmony and figured bass, and now a new system: tuning, or temperament. Pythagoras helped us a long time ago by working out the mathematical relationship of pure fifths, but nature has thrown us all a curve ball. If we tune everything perfectly according to Pythagoras, it just does not fit into the octave. Music composed for instruments, particularly keyboard, is becoming more dominant, and tuning is becoming a big problem. Think karaoke-bar-after-a-few-shandies sort of quality — things just sound a little bit off.

To explain, this is where we combine music with pandemics. To be specific, buying twelve mega-saver packs of loo roll.

Okay, here's your conundrum. You have the twelve packs (each one is a semitone note in your octave), and you need to fit them in your cupboard (your octave). You start putting them in neatly, but you reach the last pack and you realise there isn't enough room. What to do? You can't leave it out, so you shove the other packs in super tight; you shove and shove, and there! You've done it! You have now created equal temperament. Maybe not for your own temperament, but in music. Perfectly equal spaces between your notes, or loo rolls, don't come in for another hundred years, but at least now some rolls are closer together than others so you can squeeze them all in, and that is called well-tempered; this is the tuning that Bach used in his forty-eight pieces for *The Well-Tempered Clavier*. (That's why there are forty-eight chapters in this book.) Little did you know it was all about loo rolls.

And that will lead us neatly, if a bit squishedly, to a meeting with Rameau in Paris. If you order his treatise now, you might have it in time for Christmas.

Now where are those loo rolls …

Jean-Philippe Rameau, Pieces for Clavecin (Harpsichord) with a Method for the Mechanics of the Fingers

Here he is, Jean-Philippe Rameau, taking a rest from composing one of his latest operas and going for a walk in the Tuileries Garden in Paris. His coat is threadbare and his shoes are not exactly well-heeled, while Rameau himself is extremely tall and two-dimensionally thin, a narrow face rigid against the world. 'His heart and soul were in his harpsichord; once he had shut its lid, there was no-one home.' Hardly a heart-warming description of Rameau from one of his so-called friends, but apparently this is the character of Rameau — truculent, uncommunicative, a loner.

But can you blame him? Here is a man who has worked slavishly as an organist in the provinces, taking over his dad's job as François Couperin did. All the while he develops his composition and theory of harmony, and it is only when he is in his fifties, so practically dead by 1700s standards, that he hits the musical jackpot with his operas. You might be a tad stern if you've been ignored for most of your life. If you have teenage children, that may be how you're feeling right now. Speaking of children, Rameau has four with his wife but also treats his music as his children, pouring his life and love into these pocket pieces. Some of them are barely a minute long, but they are little universes of ideas, moods, gestures and dance. As a gift to go along with the music, Rameau, who never quite gets around to writing his own harpsichord for dummies manual, includes here some written instruction on how to play the instrument: 'the faculty of walking or running comes from the suppleness of the knee; that of playing the harpsichord depends on the suppleness of the fingers at their roots.' And there for the first time the knee is mentioned in music history. Rameau goes on to say how you should lightly stroke the keyboard and never be too heavy with your touch. It really is an ode to love.

Rameau gets himself embroiled in a few arguments in his time. You remember the 1600s Twitter trolls, the pamphleteers who criticised Monteverdi? Rameau has the same problem with his opera style, which people feel is too far removed from foot-banging (not head-banging) Lully. And what does he do? Exactly what Monteverdi does: tells everyone to get stuffed. In French. He also has a barney with Rousseau, the great writer and philosopher. Don't **** with these musicians.

Anticipating Arvo Pärt in three centuries to come, Rameau has his own period of composing silence for six years. And at the end of it all, at the end of his life, he wishes he didn't work in a world where imagination is everything, because his imagination has nothing left.

After all Rameau has done for our music, even geniuses come to a final cadence.

15

The public going for baroque

London, 1672. Much of the city is still in ruins after the Great Fire of 1666 and change is in the air.

Not just from the builders for Christopher Wren but from a certain Mr John Banister. Banister has recently been royal violinist to King Charles II (until he is kicked out for complaining about French musicians in the English band, that is), but Banister is about to make history in a different way. Who cares about playing for royalty if you can have money and fame by playing for the general public?

Well, general public might be a push, as tickets for these first public concerts cost a shilling, which is a late seventeenth-century financial term for an arm and a leg. But still, as London is being rebuilt after the Great Fire and society is rebuilding from the bubonic plague, for the first time ever the public can listen to music without needing to go to church or suck up to a duchess. Also for the first time ever, the public can hear good music on their own terms. And not only on their own terms — they can also choose the music, so no more sitting through endless cantatas or fusty motets. The audience might choose some of the latest musical items, especially concertos (more about them in the next chapter), mix them up with an aria or two with the most famous diva of the time, then maybe wrap the three-hour concert up with a dramatic bit of storytelling, called an oratorio, by Handel. It's popular music and André Rieu would not be out of place here.

In England in the early 1700s, the Academy of Ancient Music puts on concerts of music from the century before (so not that ancient) and in Paris the Concert Spirituel is founded by a chap called Anne — Anne Danican Philidor, brother of a famous chess player. Anne puts on Corelli's Christmas Concerto for his first gig but goes bankrupt within two years. Well, you can't blame it on the music, but you can blame it on the king, as paying the royal licence puts too much strain on the business model. Once the king stops charging a licence fee the concerts flourish, until Monsieur Guillotine comes to a square near you with his macabre contraption and the French Revolution changes everything. By then, everything in music has changed anyway. Now the virtuosity of the performer is paramount, and that leads nicely to our next story: the rise, and rise, and rise again (right up to a precipitous top E) of the violin.

Arcangelo Corelli, Twelve Concerti Grossi

Arcangelo Corelli, master melodist, perfectionist and violinist extraordinaire, by one account doesn't start playing the fiddle until he is about thirteen years old. Virtually past it by some standards. That doesn't seem to matter as Corelli goes on to become one of the great virtuosos of his age and one of the most influential musicians in history. This guy is the Coco Chanel of the music world: timeless, stylish, faultless.

If you are going to go to any concert in the early 1700s you would really want to save up to see Corelli. Great violinists can be judged by how many gazillion notes they can play a second, but Corelli is different. Corelli makes the sweetest sound imaginable on his violin. It's so sweet, you can taste it. Unusually for the time, Corelli writes nothing for the voice and almost exclusively for string instruments, and then only in three different styles: trio sonatas, sonatas for solo instruments and concerti grossi.

What?

Concerti grossi, or, if there is only one, concerto grosso.

So you remember sonatas (literally 'to sound', as opposed to cantata, 'to sing'), which come from part of the Catholic mass? Trio sonatas are for two violins, cello and keyboard. Corelli, in another of the sliding-door moments in music history, says one day, 'What about if I keep the two violins and cello as the lead group and give the music I'd play on the keyboard to a bunch of other string players instead?' And, ta-da, the concerto grosso is born. The lead group is called the concertino, which sounds like a delicious coffee, and the support act is called the ripieno, which sounds like a delicious ice cream. So the stars, the concertino, are belting out the tune at the front, and the chorus, the ripieno, is up the back as the support act. This is music with built-in tension as the tune gets passed to and fro between the groups. Think Sharks and Jets from *West Side Story*, with bows and curls instead of knives and slick.

Corelli composes a bunch of sonatas and only twelve concerti grossi. But these twelve, they are a wondrous galaxy. Corelli's music goes on to influence Bach, George Handel, Domenico Scarlatti, and Michael Tippett and Igor Stravinsky in the twentieth century. Corelli, with his new dynamic range of louds and softs, and his deep understanding of harmony and the potential beauties and hazards of going from one chord to the next, takes us down an avenue of safety, surprise, deep satisfaction and astonishment. How can the sounds of harmony, these major and minor scales, change our mood, our prospects, our perspective? This is not just well-built music — this is music that will survive the onslaught of history and be studied by music students in hundreds of years' time. Here is a jamboree, a jubilee of music, cavorting, skipping and dancing like no-one is watching.

Corelli, you could say, has nailed it. Just like Martin Luther.

16

The violin

It is made from seventy different pieces of wood, held together with animal glue and played with horsehair pulled tight over a sprung stick. Its wood is sourced from high mountain valleys and felled when the moon is dark so the wood is as sap-free and resonant as possible. It is an instrument that inspires the most ardent emotions, and classical music is almost unimaginable without it.

From its beginning in the 1500s, developed from various instruments including the Arabian rebab and the mediaeval vielle (remember the drone with Hildegard of Bingen?), how did the violin and other instruments in the family, the viola, cello and double bass, come to dominate music throughout Europe?

The answer may lie in the world around it.

Technology in the eighteenth century is making life go faster — the invention of the water-powered cotton mill, the spinning jenny and the flying shuttle all industrialise weaving, and the invention of modern steel and precision lathes bring the

Industrial Revolution into sight. Those days of sitting back in a paddock waiting for the sun to go down are about to change to a life of strict timetables and efficiency.

And political acts bring bigger dominions — the union of Scotland and England, violent colonisation of the Americas and the evil growth of the slave trade from Africa, with wars between European countries as well. The eighteenth century is very much about more and more, bigger and bigger possession, speed, volume and, yes, greed.

So as public concerts start in 1672, that desire for more music, more virtuosity and more volume aligns perfectly with the development of the violin. The design of the violin, with makers like Amati, Stradivarius and Guadagnini, is perfected so quickly in the seventeenth century that it has hardly changed for the last four hundred years. The violin, with its four strings as opposed to six on a viola da gamba, its ability to be played standing up and its brighter, louder sound, is perfect for these strident times. The four strings allow for a single line to be spun more effectively, as opposed to the more chordal sound of the viola da gamba. This is a modern sound. This is the sound of the conqueror.

The violin's bigger sibling, the cello, also has a technological growth spurt, with string makers working out how to cover gut strings with metal to produce a clearer sound for the lower notes. The cello changes from an instrument where you can barely hear the bottom (in other circumstances that's a good thing) to an instrument that gradually assumes the mantel of the hero of the orchestra and will be an inspiration for J.S. Bach in some of the most famous music ever written, his six *Cello Suites*.

Composers develop music forms to match the change in speed. Concertos (developed from the concerto grosso) — from the Italian meaning to bring into agreement, or, confusingly, possibly also meaning a conflict (well, there's been a few of them in performance) — are ideal for showing off players' skills. In the new age of individuality and celebrating the soloist, concertos mirror opera and the aria with extreme expressiveness and fancy-pants showing off.

It may have taken a few hundred years but those days of monks singing in unison are long gone. Now, with the Enlightenment just around the corner, music is more and more about freedom of expression and the individual over the collective.

And those forests where Stradivari and Guarneri and Amati found their wood? They are in the Fiemme Valley, the foothills of the Italian Alps, and you can visit the forest still if you take the B104 bus from Trento.

Giuseppe Torelli, Violin Concerto in D Minor

You remember those skittish monks mucking around with a drone six hundred years ago, who gave us the first harmony? And Corelli deciding to give some unemployed string players the music he was playing on the keyboard, which gave us the first concerto grosso? With Giuseppe Torelli we have a similar moment, but now a violinist is playing with a cellist one day and then heads off on their own into a lengthy solo. Like question time in parliament, where the opposition is hogging the limelight and all you can do is shout a bit from the back. This moment is the beginning of an ego trip like no other: the solo concerto.

Torelli plays violin and viola (big violin, small cello or just a joke, please take your pick) and, like most composers around this time, makes his money with various gigs for the nobility and the church. This new sound he has created, with one voice singing over the top of many others, is the sound of life. How often must people, particularly the non-nobility, wish they could be heard? Now they have a sound to represent a life they can dream of, a life where they are in charge. With the concerto, everyman/woman is fighting back. One violinist-composer to come in a few decades, Maddalena Lombardini Sirmen, will use her violin as a force through the world, beginning to establish a place for women on the concert platform and as respected composers.

Torelli eventually composes more concertos for the trumpet than the violin; he must be doing something right because his music is transcribed by none other than Johann Sebastian himself.

And speaking of Bach …

17

J.S.B.

Northern Germany, October 1705. A path high in the Harz Mountains, winding through sycamore and oak, beech and silver birch. The ground hard with frost, a young man's boots striking rhythmically against the earth and the silence. A young man walking to his future.

The man, twenty years old, is on a long journey, walking four hundred and fifty kilometres through the rain and cold to hear one of the great organists of his age, Dieterich Buxtehude. As he walks, the young man thinks of his family, six generations of musicians, of his older brother, who raised him and taught him music when they were orphaned, and of his current job, playing organ in the small town of Arnstadt.

As the man walks he dreams of his future — possibly moving to a town with a better choir (the choir director in Arnstadt likes wine more than singing), maybe working with more skilful musicians (the young man has already had a street fight with a bassoonist about his poor playing) — and of the music he will compose, music that will combine the rhythms of the French, the melody of the Italians and the complexity of the Germans to create a perfect language. You could say that everything in music so far, all the way from the Sumerians and Ancient Greeks through the early church chanting and the slow evolution of harmony from drones to polyphony, synthesises in this man, walking through the silent woods, whistling his latest tune.

Because this young man is Johann Sebastian Bach, and his music will survive a lull to be resurrected by Felix Mendelssohn and played and exalted for the next three hundred years. Johann Sebastian Bach will go on to produce hundreds of works, sacred and secular, for solo instruments and the full glory of choir and orchestra, music that illustrates the breadth of the church calendar and our own human experience.

Bach's life is one of determination and hard work. Unimaginable hard work. His commitment to his artistry will have him thrown in jail for trying to leave one job, brought up before church councils for pushing the boundaries in another and having endless arguments with small-minded officials who simply want him to play less complex music.

Whether it is Bach's joyful dance suites, his virtuosic *Brandenburg Concertos* or the work described as the zenith of Western art, *St Matthew Passion*, Bach's music describes life in all its counterpoint complexity.

In contrast with this earthbound journey the young man now takes, walking from Arnstadt to Lübeck, Bach's music will be placed in the Voyager space capsule and sent to the stars.

J.S. Bach, Brandenburg Concerto No. 6 in B-flat Major, BWV 1051

When you want to leave a job, perhaps you unconsciously begin by upsetting the status quo — maybe coming in to work a bit later, delaying projects, questioning more decisions. So you'll understand what Johann Sebastian Bach is up to here in Köthen; Bach really wants a new gig.

Working in Köthen has its benefits — skilled musicians, lots of financial support — but wouldn't working for the younger brother of the king be even better? To provoke some change, Bach writes a concerto and puts the prince's instrument, the viola da gamba, into the supporting act and his own instrument, the viola, as the star. As double stars, in fact. This is impudent stuff.

The reason Bach is doing all this is simple: he has recently travelled to Berlin to buy himself a new harpsichord and maybe a new hat, and while there he bumps into a guy called Christian Ludwig, the Margrave of Brandenburg and, most importantly, the king's younger brother. Christian seems to like Bach's playing, so Bach takes the opportunity and sends him a set of six concertos for various instruments and basically asks him for a job. He even copies the music out himself rather than trust someone else to do it. When you read 'takes the opportunity', Bach does in fact wait a couple of years — maybe something happened to push Bach into wanting to leave, maybe he didn't want anyone to know he was essentially applying for a new gig, or maybe he was just too busy to do it any earlier.

Bach's package of music is completely ignored, despite an obsequious letter from Bach to Christian. How terrible that

such a genius as Bach must virtually beg for any attention from this guy. Not even a polite 'thanks for your note …' from the Margrave. It gets worse. The six concertos are dumped into a job lot with other pieces by third-rate composers and stuffed on a shelf at the back of the music library for the next hundred years. This is the musical equivalent of that kitchen drawer where you keep dead lighters, dead biros and dead batteries. The scores end up in the Brandenburg state archive and this is where two heroic librarians take centre stage, thanks to a bank collapse and a British bomber.

Please enter, library aisle left, Siegfried Dehn. He was to have been a lawyer, but Dehn's family's bank collapse has him realise he should be living his dream, so he becomes a music theorist and teacher, and in 1842, at the age of forty-three, he is put in charge of the Prussian royal library. This guy is diligent. With a capital 'D'. He goes through everything at the library letter by letter, and by the time 1849 rolls around he has reached the letter 'M' for music and discovers these six concertos. It's the cultural equivalent to discovering Tutankhamun's tomb, relics from ancient China, the glasses you lost last week. This is an autographed original manuscript, a cultural gemstone of the world by one of the great geniuses in history. No wonder this music is on the Voyager spacecraft.

Siegfried Dehn sends the music out into the world, but it's not until the 1930s that it is performed more widely. At least by now there are a few other copies, so please welcome, mid-World War 2 and train aisle left, another heroic librarian. This person's name is not known, so let's call her Anna. Anna has accompanied a stash of important items from the Brandenburg archive being taken by train away from the Allied bombings. The artifacts include these six concertos, which by now have acquired the nickname the *Brandenburg Concertos*. War being war, the train is bombed and Anna escapes into the woods, clutching Bach's autographed manuscript inside her coat. Those same manuscripts that were written out by Bach, sent in the mail by Bach and left for a hundred and more years on a shelf by someone who didn't realise it was Bach are now in the middle of an air raid and they barely survive.

After all this, we have the deepest privilege of being able to hear what Bach wanted us to hear.

Here Bach is, standing next to us as we listen, nodding appreciatively, possibly wondering whether that job with the Margrave would have been any good, after all; it's a moot point. Bach knows the most important thing: he composed superlative music because of it, and maybe that is enough.

18

~~Jet~~ Cart-setters

Road surfaces and princesses. They seem unlikely contributions to music, but here in the 1700s, the music we are listening to depends on the quality of both.

Okay, let's talk about the roads first. From the beginning of the century, advances in road building, basically from mud to stone, mean travel times are drastically reduced. Higher quality toll roads allow people to move around more quickly and more safely. Which means we can go exploring.

The Grand Tour, a rite of passage undertaken by wealthy twenty-somethings (mostly men), expands musical taste and desire. Combine this with increased publishing of opinion (think Instagram with oil colours) and it opens up a whole new market for musicians. No longer do you have to stay in your home town and hope the person who holds the job you want dies soon. Now, like the composers Scarlatti and Porpora and Geminiani, you can go to a new country, combine your style of music with theirs, and create a whole new vogue, an international style.

One guy called Charles Burney, from Shropshire in England, visits European royal courts and fancy houses to meet musicians (think of him as an early *Rolling Stone* correspondent) and spreads the word and the music, so travelling musicians in Europe become more common than non-travelling ones. Johann Sebastian Bach, who doesn't travel more than five hundred kilometres in his life, is the exception not the rule. Georg Handel, in contrast, travels from Germany to Italy and England. These people are international jetsetters. No, cart-setters.

Europe is made even more international by royal marriage — Spanish kings in Naples, a German princess (Catherine the Great) in Russia, and German kings in England. The German composer Georg Philipp Telemann celebrates with a collection of music called *The Nations*, a mashup of European dances.

All this cart-setting has a downside, though.

Georg Friedrich Handel is another man with itchy feet. So itchy that at twenty-one he travels from northern Germany to Rome, and from there back to the Electorate of Hannover and a short stint working for the elector, another Georg, a post he abandons to move to London. Handel may well be cursing the intermarriage of European royal families, as that elector he abandons becomes King George I in England. Royal George thankfully doesn't hold a grudge and embraces Handel, now George Frederic (rather than Georg Frideric), as the musical golden boy of England. Think Harry Styles with a wig.

So much travel and cross-fertilisation of music styles and human DNA brings a new sound that is no longer limited by international borders. Now it's the sound of Europe.

George Frederic Handel, *Water Music*

George Frederic Handel is the quintessential bewigged man about town in London in the 1700s. He has come a long way from his childhood in Halle, where his dad refused to allow him to learn music so baby George had to play his clavichord in secret. Quite how he got the clavichord up the stairs is another matter. Anyway, now he is famous, he is rich, he is socially well connected, he has aristocratic patrons and possibly some lovers as well, but the one thing he doesn't have (yet) is a good relationship with the king. That's another George — the First, with a capital fir. The reason for this is that George Handel had worked for Other George already in Hanover but then deserted that court and came over to England. And now the boss there is the boss in England. The boss *of* England. You'd be a bit embarrassed too if you'd skipped town for a better job and your old boss is now your new one. Whoops. George Handel is in luck, though. Other George, now King George, is not very popular with the Brits: first, he's German, and second, he's not very smart or good-looking, so he desperately needs a lift in the polls. And what better way to get everyone to like you than by throwing a party!

And this isn't just any old party. King George decides to make the River Thames his disco hall and a flotilla of barges the movable furniture. He then asks Handel, who is by now the more popular of the two Georges, to compose music they can all listen to as they sail up the Thames and then down again. It seems like this is the royal pardon George H has been waiting for.

Handel's *Water Music* is a collection of European dances: hornpipes from Britain, gigas and airs from Italy, sarabandes from Spain, bourées, minuets and rigadoons from France. The music is short and snappy, and although the dances all have international origins there is still a sturdiness and stockiness to the rhythms that is quintessentially English. And the English go nuts for it. The Thames is thick with boats and crowds wanting to come to the social occasion of the decade. Just think of the clean-up the next morning.

And just think of those poor musicians. Fifty of them, with horn players coming specially from Italy, wind players, string players, all crowded onto a barge, all trying to find enough room to play, trying to watch the conductor (who is Handel himself) and not feel seasick, and making sure the wind doesn't blow their music away. On top of all that, the musicians need to keep playing until midnight. Again and again, for three hours up the river and maybe a bit shorter coming down, depending on the tide. Let's hope they are paid at least union rates and have some time off in lieu. And time off in the loo.

19

Are you enlightened yet?

'Hello! Welcome to the Zimmerman Café here in Leipzig, where Johann Sebastian is just warming up — he's sounding pretty good already, though, don't you think? The gig starts at two, so would you like a coffee? Flat white?'

It's 1735 and, okay, flat whites may not have reached the cafés of Europe, but who needs flat whites when you now have so many other stimulants? Newspapers are cheaper and more widespread, and as you are now more likely to be literate, since public schools are improving, you can also read journals and diaries (otherwise known as eighteenth-century blogs) about the latest gossip, wars, executions and concerts.

For the first time, people — well, the middle classes — throughout Europe are expressing their opinions about everything. And their individual rights are being championed by social reformers like Voltaire and Rousseau (just not when he's arguing with Rameau). A new thinking is developing, a movement we now know as the Enlightenment. Reason is foremost; reason and direct experience to evaluate the world.

Taste becomes an argument between the social classes, a 1700s culture war, with the middle classes wanting simplicity and candid emotion. They also want music to represent nature as society is becoming more urbanised. They want music to portray *their* lives, not just the lives of fancy-pants royals.

Culture is now very much within the reach of all, with a public baying for new music, so musicians need to keep up. Never have composers been more prolific, with Georg Philipp Telemann alone writing close to a thousand different works.

But how does all this influence the sound of music? Great question.

Okay, let's consider the opening to Johann Sebastian Bach's work *St John Passion*. You can hear how the music is in many layers, like a vanilla slice, with the oboes lying on top, several layers of music below and everything held up by the cellos and basses. There isn't exactly a tune, yet this is baroque music in all its complex glory.

But if you now listen to Christoph Willibald Gluck's aria 'Che farò senza Euridice?', you can hear the brightness and clarity, an obvious melody over the top of accompaniment. This growing sense of style in opera spreads to other spaces, and instrumental music begins to change; it is more and more influenced by that glory of glories deep within our bodies — our voice. The world of opera, where music is composed with breath and words and sentences in mind, brings that cadence and sense to all music. The new style, called 'galant' or 'rococo'

or *Empfindsamkeit*, is clear, logical and with a tune you can whistle over your coffee.

It's somehow apt that in a world where the individual is having their voice heard more and more, music's inspiration is that very voice.

Christoph Willibald Gluck, 'What Will I Do Without Euridice?'

Here he is, Christoph Willibald, taking a break from opera rehearsals and off for a walk in the Tuileries Garden in Paris, just like Rameau but better dressed and with a vanilla ice cream. Gluck has just been invited to Paris by a woman called Marie Antoinette — you may have heard of her. Marie Antoinette was a (presumably music) student of Gluck's and is so impressed with his new operas that she has invited him to live in the city of light. Maybe if he plays his cards and clavichord right, he'll get an invite to Versailles for a slice of gâteau. Yum.

Gluck is a reformer. And no, nothing to do with Pilates. Gluck is developing a whole new style of opera that will eventually be called reform opera, because up to now the whole schtick of opera has been, let's say, lengthy and repetitive. With Gluck, the story is now paramount instead of the singers and their fancy arias (this will eventually catch on with musicals in the twentieth century). And now the orchestra plays all the way through the action, just like a film soundtrack, giving the whole concept clarity and conciseness. Gluck's new operas are about half as long as those serious operas by people like Handel and Vivaldi, and Gluck's ideas of revealing emotion and action are so powerful that, just like the design of the violin is so perfect it hasn't changed, Gluck's opera ideas stay all the way through to Wagner and Verdi.

With this aria we are towards the end of the opera, which is thankfully after one hour instead of three, and Orpheus is singing to himself, 'Bugger, I wish I'd listened to that bloke and hadn't looked around at Euridice. What am I going to do without her?'

When it's first written, this aria is performed by a man who has been castrated, called a castrato. (Well, his name might be Bobby, but his body is called a castrato.) Nowadays, as you breathe a sigh of relief in a deep voice, we hear either a woman or a man singing very high because they naturally can, while keeping all their body parts as well. The aria is given a brief introduction by the violins with the sorrowful tune and then Orpheus enters singing exactly the same tune. Nothing fancy, but the melody is the essence of regret and dismay as it attempts to float up and then inevitably falls back down to earth. Doom propels itself from the wind players as Orpheus wonders whether he can even walk on and leave Hades. And, to drive home the point about reform opera being a simpler form, even the lyrics are simple; Orpheus repeats the chorus three times with very short verses between. Gluck really knows how to bring a good tune home. If only Orpheus could do the same thing with Euridice.

20

The loudsoft

We have gone backwards a bit (just like John Lennon in 'Rain') from the mid-1700s to 1688, but there's a good reason. You need to shine your shoe buckles and powder your wig because we are going to one of the Medici palaces in Florence for a job interview with Prince Ferdinando.

This guy isn't one of those princes who just feeds off the poor and does his nails all day; Ferdinando is a brilliant musician and serious patron of the arts. He is building a ... fleet? of instruments, which includes over seventy harpsichords. When you have so many instruments you need someone to look after them, hence the job interview, so welcome harpsichord left Bartolomeo Cristofori, thirty-three years old, from Padua.

Not only does Ferdinando want a caretaker for the old instruments, he also wants designs for whole new instruments.

Cristofori does not disappoint. In 1700 there is an indisputable entry in the Medici inventory of 'an "arpicembalo" by Bartolomeo Cristofori, a new invention that produces soft and loud'.

The new keyboard instrument is indeed called an arpicembalo, literally harp-harpsichord, but because it can now play loud and soft (in Italian, *forte* and *piano*) everyone ignores the inventor and calls it a fortepiano, which, just as we reduce words in Australia to budgie, arvo and barbie, is later shortened from fortepiano to just piano. Mate.

But what's the big deal, you ask? Why don't we just stick with that quiet clavichord that Handel played on in the attic so his grumpy dad couldn't hear him, or the slightly louder harpsichord that Johann Sebastian Bach is playing right now back in Germany?

The answer is responsiveness and range. With plucked instruments like the harpsichord, there is no variety in dynamic. But now, with a variation you can achieve with a hammer (that sounds like a bad joke), this new instrument can play a huge range of dynamics, building on the sound Corelli started a few decades back. A new music is developing, a music of extreme emotions and sensitivity, and the arpicembalo, sorry, fortepiano, is the perfect instrument for showing your sensitive side as a musician with its new-fangled way of producing a sound.

Before now, keyboards have used a plucking mechanism which, unless you're Carlos Santana, has its limits in tonal variation. With the mechanism invented by Cristofori, the strings are now hammered with an action that stops them being dampened and also prevents the hammer bouncing back; a jack silences the string when it's not being played and there's a more resonant soundboard. As the Industrial Revolution brings stronger materials, the fortepiano becomes bigger and louder, with more keys and more possibilities.

The first music written specifically for the fortepiano is a sonata by Ludovico Giustini. You can hear the sound is still quiet by modern standards, but there's more of a sustain to the melody; it's a sweeter sound.

Princess Maria Bárbara in Spain gives fortepianos to the composer Domenico Scarlatti, who writes his keyboard sonatas for the instrument. So now we have gone from virginals to clavichord to harpsichord to fortepiano, and in a century or two we will be hearing the same music played on a grand piano weighing half a tonne. It's a good job Handel doesn't have to sneak one of those into his attic.

Bach's youngest son, Johann Christian, is one of those jet/cart-setting musicians who moves from Germany to London and plays the fortepiano in public for the first time, using a knee lever for the sustaining pedal. And for the second time, the knee makes its way into music history.

Domenico Scarlatti, Sonata for Keyboard in D Minor, K141

You'll be getting the picture by now that many of our composers come from musical families, and that they are writing music and performing from a very young age. Think Bach and his five generations of musicians before him, or Couperin taking on his dad's job as an organist at the age of eleven. Which seems a little precocious, but there isn't the distraction of video games.

Domenico's dad is called Alessandro (Scarlatti, no surprise) and he composes opera, Italian overtures (more of them later), the earliest string quartets, and is generally important for creating forms of music such as the type of aria that Gluck reforms. So thanks, Alessandro, and thanks for trying to get your son a gig in Florence with one of the Medici princes. You didn't succeed, but there's a classic 'I'm going to get out of this' letter from the prince that basically says, 'This dude is brilliant and can get a gig anywhere, so I'm not going to be bothered helping him.' Thanks for nothing. But the prince is correct, because Domenico goes ahead and triumphs throughout Europe, playing for an exiled princess here, a marquis there, and even ending up in a keyboard duel with George Handel! (This is one of the few exclamation marks in this book, and surely this is the place for it.) There isn't a clear winner, but dear Scarlatti gives the organ-playing prize to Handel.

After quite a few to's and fro's throughout Europe, Scarlatti ends up in Spain, working for, you guessed it, a princess from Portugal who loves music and especially loves the new-fangled fortepiano. Princess Maria Bárbara, now married to the crown prince of Spain, can afford to indulge herself and her favourite composer with a few fortepianos, and that's exactly what she does, ending up with five of them by the end of her life. What do you do with five? Have a fortepiano party? Anyhoo, this means that Scarlatti is kept busy writing five hundred and fifty-five sonatas for the instrument. That's a hundred and eleven for each one. Curiously the sonatas are grouped into collections of thirty. Why? Is it a religious reference to Jesus Christ being baptised when he is thirty? Or a convenient number for learning one each day for a month? There's your next challenge, and you'll have your work cut out for you in February.

This little gem, lasting three and a quarter minutes, is tucked in the middle somewhere, and it's completely outrageous. Forget those harpsichords where the mechanism slows the playing down. Now, with this advanced technology and whacking the string with a hammer instead of plucking, you can blast off into the stratosphere as fast as you dare.

21

Life is a symphony

So you may have noticed here in the latter part of the 1700s that the biggest influence in music in Europe so far is ... The Voice! Yes, the TV show. Guy Sebastian especially.

Oh okay, not the TV *Voice*. But certainly the human voice and opera. You remember that new galant style of music, a good whistle-able tune over some accompaniment? This is now not only in opera but also played on instruments in sonatas (although some people, notably Jean-Jacques Rousseau, are complaining about this new instrumental music, saying it's short on substance — ouch).

From the opera world, there's another huge wind blowing your way (not the tuba, that hasn't been invented yet) — the symphony. Sure, we have had that word used before for various pieces, including the Sacred Symphonies by Gabrieli, but now it's different.

Operas have had instrumental introductions for years. After all, you need something to listen to as you fight for your seat, arrange your hosiery, gossip about the latest scandal and warm up your ears for the famous castrato singer. These opera introductions are called sinfonias (or Italian overtures), literally 'sounding together'; Alessandro Scarlatti is a big fan. The sinfonias, with their three segments at different speeds, are gradually turned into longer pieces by other Italian composers, especially one dude, Giuseppe Sammartini. His name does sound like a glamorous version of a martini, but yes, he's definitely a composer.

Sammartini works for the Catholic church around Milan and takes the opera sinfonia and similar ideas from concertos and baroque orchestral suites to create little symphonies inside the Catholic mass. Think of them like commercials in your favourite TV show.

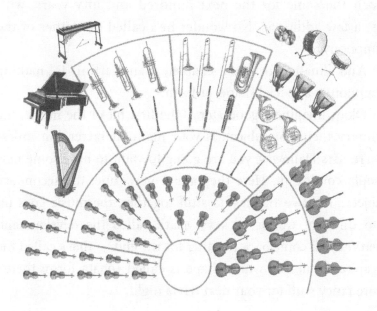

Initially Sammartini writes symphonies for strings with a harpsichord as well. You remember Lully and his letting the brass out of the stables for the first orchestras? Sammartini has the similar notion and removes the harpsichord (this is an old-fashioned sound by now) and adds horns to the strings.

So now we have strings and horns, zero harpsichord, and the orchestra is led by the tallest violinist. Or the best. Or the one with the nicest wig. Hmm, maybe all three. As Sammartini goes on with his work (he writes seventy symphonies all up) he adds not only horns but also wind instruments to the orchestra. When you have all these instruments play together, you can hear the sound has moved a long way from the intricacies of the baroque. It's refined, it's delicate and, yes, it's full of light and shade. Sammartini creates a timbre that will stay pretty much the same for the next hundred and fifty years, with just a few additions. No wonder he's called the father of the symphony.

And finally for this chapter, Sammartini is making symphonies a special shape, or form.

Okay, imagine a good story. The first bit of the music, the primary theme or subject, is your main character, but unless you're Mrs Dalloway, you are going to want to have some new people coming in. Here they are: a new tune, the secondary subject. The two themes do stuff together, the music goes off into different worlds or keys, that's called the development, then they all come back together for the end — that's called the recapitulation. The whole shape is called sonata form; there's more fancy stuff for your next trivia night.

The Mannheim composer Johann Stamitz makes symphonies even more thrilling with spurts of soft to **loud** (crescendos), dubbed the Mannheim ro**cket**. And Joseph Haydn, just recently awarded a big gig at Esterházy Palace in 1761, will compose one hundred and four symphonies and invent a whole new sound — the string quartet. It's a heady time to be alive, although speaking of heads, revolution is just around the corner ...

Johann Stamitz, Symphony in D Major

Wow. If you've been listening to this music sequentially all the way from the Ancient Greeks, nothing will prepare you for this sound, not even Bach's *Brandenburg Concertos*. This symphony, with its horns, flutes, oboes, bassoons and strings, is a sonic eruption inside your head. Here is music as pure celebration in D major, the key of war cries and victory.

Johann Stamitz is a viola player (btw, all the best composers are: Bach, Haydn, Mozart, Beethoven, Schubert, Dvořák, Resphighi, Britten, Jimi Hendrix ...) and he sees the world from the middle of music, where the violas play. It would be like climbing inside an engine and watching the spark plugs spark and the pistons pist, being able to smell the source of momentum. Johann changes the sound of the symphony, and his use of musical energy with his new crescendos and diminuendos and all this dashing colour and light peals through the centuries to Gioachino Rossini, Georges Bizet, Sergei Prokofiev and Anna Pavlova. When the musicologist Charles Burney comes to visit Stamitz's Mannheim orchestra from Shropshire, he describes it as 'an army of generals, equally fit to plan a battle as to fight it'. And another guy (they have a lot of visitors) is rapturous about the band: 'Its forte is like thunder; its crescendo like a mighty waterfall; its diminuendo a gentle river disappearing into the distance; its piano a breath of spring.' Crikey. When's their next gig?

Johann Stamitz dies in 1757 at the shockingly young age of thirty-nine, leaving behind two sons who also become viola players and composers. Mannheim is the place to be because six years later someone called Nannerl Mozart and her brother Wolfgang will come to visit. They and Johann would have had a lot to talk about.

22

A good violinist, a not-so-good violinist, someone who used to be a violinist, and someone who hates violinists

'Hello, and welcome to the Esterhazy Palace! You're a bit late — did you have trouble with your horse? You'll have to park your carriage over there, sorry — this is stop, drop and go only.

'The concert has already started, so you'd better sneak in the back. Haydn is up there with his mates; they're playing one of his quartets, I think it's called the 'Sunrise', then there's something called a 'Farewell' symphony. I did see them doing it last week. They all disappeared into a broom cupboard. Very odd. I think some of them are still there.'

Here in 1772, groups with four musicians have been around for a while already. And you'll find that number sticks around throughout history — *The Golden Girls*, Dave Brubeck, DNA, Connect 4, Teenage Mutant Ninja Turtles and musicians of all backgrounds seem to work well in groups of four. We've heard motets in four voices, viol consorts with four players, and trio sonatas with two violins and a bass continuo, which is two people, so really a trio sonata is not a great description. Anyhoo, moving on ...

Jean-Baptiste Lully, boss of music for France's Sun King, already uses string ensembles, so all it takes is a few to call in sick one day for the group to be reduced to its essence: two violins, one viola, one cello. Gregorio Allegri, the guy whose 'Miserere' piece is so exquisite it is kept secret in the Sistine Chapel until wunderkind Mozart comes along and writes it down from hearing it once (gawd, some people), has written a sinfonia for the same combo, but it's Alessandro Scarlatti (remember Domenico's dad?) who gives each player more of a challenge and starts to establish the quartet sound. It's perfect for the middle classes — they can play together (well, if they can find a viola player) and show off to their heart's content without having some noisy singer or fortepiano player getting in the way.

Joseph Haydn is the composer who really certifies and develops the quartet sound. Because Haydn works for the Esterhazy family and they are often in their palace miles away from anywhere without much to see on the TV in the evenings, the family needs something to play. Something new and exciting, not that old baroque stuff. Crikey, yawn. And something with equal voices, to mirror the changes in society (although admittedly probs not at the palace). So it is from necessity that Haydn develops the quartet, turning it from a light divertimento into some of the most dramatic, profound music of its time.

Even though the parts are more balanced, still this sort of intimacy and order in music is in opposition to what is happening outside those palace walls. During these years, the population of Europe doubles and there is a need for space and simplicity, an escape from the new hurly-burly of the world. Haydn will go on to write nearly seventy works for quartet; they are at the heart of music and at the heart of their time, because now we are very, *very* definitely in the Classical period.

This chapter's title — a good violinist, a not-so-good violinist, someone who used to be a violinist and someone who hates violinists — well, it's not always true, although viola players often play the violin at the start of their studies (a violin is easier to find) and cellists may sometimes find anything other than their fine instrument a little, shall we say, inferior. Maybe when you next meet a cellist you can ask them what they really think of violinists.

And which part does Haydn play? The one at the centre of the sound, the engine room of the quartet: the viola part. Natch. Oh, sorry — *natürlich*.

Joseph Haydn, String Quartet No. 5 in F Minor, Op. 20

Joseph Haydn is a very naughty boy. He chops off the ponytail of one of his schoolmates, persuades a bassoonist to make a sound like a fart in a symphony, and writes crazy loud music to wake up his sleepy employers. His marriage is a disaster, but his wife gives as good as she gets — she uses Haydn's manuscripts to line her pots and curl her hair. Ouch. Oh, and he's the guy who ends up with two skulls in his coffin. Phrenologists 'borrowed' his skull (they must have had the skeleton key to the grave), put a replacement in there, brought the original back and forgot to take away the replacement. The word 'numbskulls' does come to mind.

Haydn's, shall we say, colourful character radiates through his music, whether it's cheeky, bucolic or tumultuous. Here's an early Haydn quartet, his Opus 20 No. 5 in F Minor. As you can hear, each of the players has an important line; they are having a conversation, and the music is more than the sum of its parts. Even though it begins in a minor key, it's as if Haydn simply cannot keep that twinkle out of his eye. He's stern, but you know he's got a lolly behind his back that he's about to give you.

You remember we talked about the shape of symphonies, their form? Haydn uses that same sonata form in this quartet in its first movement. And you also remember the original sinfonias and their three segments all at different speeds? Haydn uses that idea as well, although he now extends those segments, or movements, to four and includes a fun dance section, the minuet and trio. The minuet will turn into the waltz in a few years, but we are waltzing ahead of ourselves.

So Haydn is a funny guy, he's full of wit and charm, but at the heart of his music there's an imploded star of seriousness. To end this quartet Haydn gives us a fugue, a type of piece where the same tune comes in the four voices, one after each other, adding counterpoint to fill it all in. (Counterpoint is the theme music upside down, or inverted, something that Arnold Schoenberg will do in about a hundred and fifty years and we will think it is too mathematical.) This fugue is almost academic writing, as if Haydn is saying, 'Well, I can make you laugh, I can make you cry, but I am a complete master and don't you forget it. Now, how can I make that bassoonist sound like they're farting?'

23

Nannerl

Welcome to the next chapter, and today we are delighted to welcome a special guest: Maria Anna Mozart, also known as Nannerl, pianist, composer and older sister of Wolfgang Amadeus Mozart.

ELB: Nannerl, welcome to the book, and thanks for taking the time to chat to our readers. So I understand you've just had another baby? 1789 is a good year!
Nannerl: Yes, that's right, Ed, I've just had a baby girl. We've named her Jeanette. Leopold was my first, but my dad took him for a couple of years because Papa wanted to make sure he had a good education from the start. I missed him so much, but he's come back now that Papa's died.
ELB: I'm so sorry about your dad ... Leopold too, right? But he must have been a pretty tough parent?
Nannerl: Well, yes — he taught music to Wolfgang and me from when we were really young, then we went on these

ridiculously long tours all over Europe. I mean, it was just awful. On one of them we were away for like three years. Sure, it was fun sometimes, well, not so much when we got typhoid … Wolfie nearly died. And you know, we missed Mama. But I suppose we made a lot of money for Papa.

ELB: Nannerl, is it true you were top of the bill over your brother for the concerts?

Nannerl: Yes, I was! [This definitely deserves an exclamation mark. How tragic that this woman has been completely silenced by the men around her.] People said really nice things about me, that I was one of the best keyboard players in Europe, but when I turned eighteen, everything changed.

ELB: Oh really? What happened?

Nannerl: Well, you know, when a girl becomes a woman in this time you must do what your papa tells you. Papa said I couldn't play on stage anymore and so I had to stop. What was the word he used? Unseemly, that's it. He said now I had to stay at home, get married and have babies.

ELB: So that's what you did?

Nannerl: Yes ... well, not straightaway. I looked after Papa for a few years. Quite a few years, in fact ... like maybe fifteen? And then I wanted to get married to this lovely guy, Franz, but Papa wouldn't let me. And then he said I could marry this guy called Johann. He was a magistrate in St Gilgen, and so we went and lived there eventually. But Johann had two wives before me who'd died, so I was looking after their five children plus Leopold and now, of course, Jeanette.

ELB: But what about your music? I mean, you were, you *are* so ... brilliant.

Nannerl: Thanks, but look, I still play my keyboard every day and I teach a little. Wolfie used to send me his new piano concertos, but we haven't spoken for a while. I haven't seen him for, I don't know, maybe six years? He's just so famous now. He did encourage me to compose, he said my music was gracious. I don't know what will happen to my music, maybe it will survive. I really hope so.

ELB: Nannerl, thank you so much for talking with me and best wishes with everything.

Nannerl: Thank you. Thanks for taking an interest in me, and not just my brother.

Since recording this interview, we have been searching for any music left by Nannerl. All we could find was this:

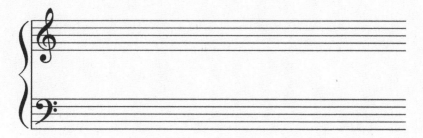

Nothing. Like so many women throughout history, Nannerl has been completely silenced.

Nannerl Mozart: In memorium

24

Talkin' 'bout a revolution

*[A] little rebellion now and then is a good thing, and as
necessary in the political world as storms in the physical.*
THOMAS JEFFERSON

France, 1789. Rising prices, staggering government debt, massive
population growth, enormous inequality and a narrow-minded
regime: it all means a revolution is just around the corner.
Thomas Jefferson is welcoming the Marquis de Lafayette and
his revolutionaries to his house in Paris for meetings where they
probably are not drinking tea and knitting. These meetings are
revolutionary with a capital rrr.

But what does revolution mean for music?

For a start, it's going to give us a seriously good tune. French
army officer Claude Joseph Rouget de Lisle is asked by the mayor
of Strasbourg to write a song that will inspire French soldiers to
fight the revolutionary fight, well, just better, and Rouget comes
up with a tune that will be whistled and sung a *lot*, especially by

volunteers in Paris from Marseille, hence the tune is called 'La Marseillaise'.

It's a song that takes the elegant style of these classical times and combines a lively tune with those famous French rhythms to create one of the first official marches. After all, how can an army do anything without a tune to move to?

When you hear of governments around the world banning music, you can understand the power of music and why people fear that power when looking at and listening to the French Revolution. Musicians are crucial to the propaganda on both sides, composing literally thousands of songs and hymns, sometimes sung at the same time on the same street. To sing in public, in a crowd, becomes an act of power and change. And the song you sing shows which side you support. In Paris, you need to be careful what you whistle and where. In 1790, François-Joseph Gossec writes a 'Te deum' hymn for the first big revolutionary festival with wind instruments and drums, the loudest and most convincing of instruments for the outdoors (remember those stable Stable jobs for Louis IV?). No mucking around with string players here — this music goes right into the rebellious ear and the defiant heart.

Before the Revolution in France, musicians were considered servants of the king, however things are about to change. Musicians contribute so much to the Revolution with performances and new pieces, but they are also broke, because their previous patrons have, er, lost their heads. A guy called Bernard Sarrette and his mates propose a new organisation, a conservatory of music funded by the state to train musicians for the future. And so it is that in April 1796 the Conservatoire de Paris opens its doors, presumably to a particularly well-played fanfare.

This school changes everything in music teaching: it has an extensive music library (where Hector Berlioz will work in a few years) and teachers develop method books for individual instruments. Up to this point, musicians would often play more than one instrument, but now the focus is more on a single instrument, which will lead to the cult of virtuosity in the nineteenth century.

So the French Revolution is not only giving us some good tunes, it's also giving us musicians with training to play those tunes better than ever. Long live the revolution in music!

Joseph Bologne, Chevalier de Saint-Georges, Symphonie Concertante in F Major

There are some people in life who just seem to have everything: physical grace and good looks, athletic ability, intelligence (emotional and the other type) and are just generally good eggs. Here's looking at you. Oh, and Joseph Bologne is also one of those people. He is known as the greatest swordsman in Europe and is a superlative violinist, athlete and marksman. He is also genteel and a spunk. Bologne's mum is an enslaved woman from Senegal, his dad is an army officer exiled from France for manslaughter, hanged in absentia then pardoned, who brings his family to France from Guadeloupe and makes sure Joseph receives an aristocratic education.

Bologne's dad is no slouch either and already has a few pieces dedicated to him, including quartets by Carl Stamitz (the Mannheim rocket man's son).

So Joseph is one of those people whose career could take them in any direction, but he chooses music and is successful as the director of the Concert des Amateurs when Gossec goes off to direct the Concert Spirituel (the orchestra that gave some of the early public concerts in Paris with that guy Anne who lost all his money). Eventually Bologne is considered for the Paris Opera top job but is denied the position because of racism. Stuff those idiots because Bologne goes on to form another orchestra, the Concert de la Loge Olympique, and they commission Joseph Haydn to write his six Paris symphonies with Bologne directing their spectacular premieres.

This is all very well, but here we are hurtling towards revolution. The Olympique band is dis-Olympique-banded, Bologne goes to England to earn money from exhibition fencing matches, then he returns to France and joins the National Guard, as the Revolution has given him equal rights as a mixed-race chap and he wants to give something back. He becomes a commander, then is denounced for 'unrevolutionary behaviour' and imprisoned for eighteen months. This brilliant man is now completely disillusioned and leaves France for St Domingue, now known as Haiti, becomes disillusioned there as well and heads back to France.

Bologne tries to re-enter the National Guard, fails, gets a gig leading a new band and abruptly dies of a bladder illness at the age of fifty-three.

Here is the life of a hero; surely there is no other character in music, apart from Clara Schumann, who faces so many adversities with so much valour.

Bologne's symphonie concertante for a couple of violins and viola is, to be honest, exceptional not because it is unusual but because it is very, very usual for its age. Despite revolution surging in the blood of the nation, this music is just so … polite. As heads are about to be chopped off and society violently reshaped, the shape of these musical phrases could hardly be milder. But that is its beauty. This music is just the right amount of predictable; it is symmetrical, elegant, refined, occasionally dashing and thrilling, but never too much. Here is the epitome of classicism, with a real mensch at its heart.

25

It's a classic

Classical style — it's something we all chase, right? The perfect black dress, a solid pair of brogues. Ooh, maybe a Canadian tuxedo and pearls. Now there's a look.

Oh, sorry, you mean classical music style? Aha. Alright, it is probably a good idea to have another look at that before we head into the next bit of our journey. Let's have a think. Here we are, on the precipice of the nineteenth century, and so, so much has changed over the last fifty years.

Now if there is one date you might like to remember in music history then it's the year of Johann Sebastian Bach's death: 1750. It's roughly around this year that music moves from the baroque into the classical period, although, as we have already learned, there are a few other styles along the way such as galant, a sort of half-step into this new fashion, like those three-quarter-length shorts fashionable in the early 2000s. But better.

If you were to sum up the classical style in a few ideas, they would be these:

Number one, a good tune with a simple accompaniment. A dude called Domenico Alberti creates a sound called — drumroll — the Alberti bass! It's a music version of glitter.

Number two, that good tune needs to have a certain formality to it, a predictable rise and fall and clear punctuation in the music. Those junctions are called cadences, and here is one. And here's another, just for fun. Cadences are full stops, or commas, in music; or semi-colons.

Number three, you remember a while ago we talked about sonata form? This, with its exposition, development and recapitulation, will impress your friends and be at the heart of symphonies and, er, sonatas.

Number four, clear dynamics, and a *lot* of contrast. Remember that Mannheim rocket? And how about a Mozart pianissimo?

Number five in our list of classical style ideas is slightly less obvious, but now, after that rush of codification of notes, rhythm and harmony, we finally have a codification of instrumentation. Doesn't that sound fancy? No more vague bass continuo that could include a cello, a bass or a bassoon, all of the above and also your father-in-law (and why not your mother-in-law as well?). Now the instruments are decided by the composer, and the bass continuo is dis-continuoed. If you are a theorbo player, you better find yourself another instrument as those gigs have dried up big time. At least you won't have to worry about how to take your instrument to the next concert anymore.

Number six, do you remember quite a while ago when together we tried squeezing your mega pack of loo rolls into the cupboard? You might recall that each loo roll is a half step, or semitone, and unless we squeeze them really hard they don't fit into our cupboard, or octave? Once they are in, that way of tuning an instrument is called equal temperament, and equal temperament has now taken over music, especially with the fortepiano. This means composers can go further with harmony, have a bolder development of keys and an even stronger definition between home and away, tension and release, the home key and other keys further away.

Number seven, to show sophistication in your composing, it's classy to include sounds from outside Europe. The great classical music traditions of Turkiye and the Arabian Peninsula are influences, with Marin Marais back in the early baroque composing arabesques, and Wolfgang Mozart and Joseph Haydn and Ludwig van Beethoven with their 'alla Turka' style in piano music and opera.

So you might say that with this classical style we have a clearer definition of where we are and where we might be going. And now that is clear, it's time for us to go on another walk. But first, a tale of a woman wronged, even after her death.

Maria Theresia von Paradis, 'Morning Song of a Pauper'

Joseph Bologne is a character so wild, you would not believe him even if you read about him in a book. Oh wait, you have just read about him in a book … It's all true, promise! Our next character, Maria Theresia von Paradis, has a similar trajectory of adventure and profound personal challenges, a pioneer in her time.

Maria, just like Joseph, has a posh dad. But that's where those similarities end. Maria's dad works for the Empress Maria Theresa and names his only child after his employer. Talk about sucking up. By the time MT is five she has become blind (no-one knows why), and is constantly treated by doctors, sometimes quacks, who do the most dreadful things to her. One man bandages her head tightly to stimulate the optic nerve, another bloke tries to electrocute her eyes. And the most famous, Franz Mesmer, manages to briefly bring back her eyesight but also believes her blindness to be part of an hysteria. Oh gosh. How women suffer.

Maria Theresia tours Europe for three years (that's a lot of hotel soap sachets) with her mum, meets many of the most famous composers and rulers of the age and begins composing music with a special peg board. She eventually settles in Vienna, starts up her own music school for girls and dedicates herself to composition. One of the few songs to survive is 'Morning Song of a Pauper' from her *Twelve Songs of Travel*. Maria Theresia's music is cutting, stoic, a baton of sound shoving you to a dreadful place. It's not surprising that the poem by Johann Hermes she sets to music is a wretched portrayal of poverty and the inevitability of misery.

There is one line where you cannot but think of Maria Theresia: 'the last thing she viewed is grief'. Here she is, a brilliant woman who has worked and worked to be able to play, compose, perform, to be free in some way, and yet always lurking in the shadows is the threat of this being taken away from her. By a man. And yet Maria Theresia composes her music with such

... composure. You feel the symmetry, the beautiful logic of her phrases going up, coming down, questioning, answering, tensing and releasing.

Nearly all the rest of Maria Theresia's music has been lost: two piano concertos, five operas, a bunch of songs and keyboard works, lost lost lost lost lost lost lost lost lost lost lost lost. Lost. And in some warped irony, the most famous work ascribed to Maria Theresia isn't written by her at all: 'The Sicilienne in E-flat Major' is an exquisite little piece that was written in the twentieth century by some bloke called Samuel Dushkin. Here is a man abusing the good name of Maria Theresia, even after her death.

26

Da-da-da-daaaaa

Heiligenstadt, 6 October 1802. A village on the outskirts of Vienna, the winter sun leaving the tops of the Vienna Woods in the late afternoon.

A man walks alone along a path, his brow clenched, hands moving as if over an imaginary keyboard, dark hair chaotic, although this chaos is a mere backdrop for his eyes — frenzied, desperate, defeated.

The man walks uphill, the sounds of the village falling behind — horse hoofs, water pumps, ironmongers, vegetable sellers, church bells, backyard chickens. He walks and walks, his head bowed. Sound is left behind as the man walks into an aural blackout.

He has come to the village on the advice of his doctor, who says the quiet might preserve some of his remaining hearing. Or it might not. Ludwig van Beethoven has known that his hearing is collapsing for many years now; he knows he can still compose but that his days of performing must soon end. Beethoven has completed a sonata in the style of a fantasy (people will later call it the 'Moonlight Sonata'), and he has just performed it here in Vienna. He composed the sonata for a young student with whom he is in love, a woman beyond his rank. She will be one among many whom he loves but knows he will never be allowed to marry.

Beethoven has grown up in the Enlightenment, an age where rights should be equal for all people. He has been taken out of school at the age of eleven to concentrate on music alone. He has studied with Joseph Haydn, who suggests he moves from Bonn to Vienna, where he is patronised by royalty. He is one of Europe's first truly freelance composers and he knows he must rely on himself alone to survive.

On this day he will return home to write a letter to his brothers, a letter in which he admits his deafness and his despair, a letter to become known as the Heiligenstadt Testament, and on this day and beyond, Beethoven will demonstrate the greatest resilience ever shown by a musician. Beethoven will decide that, because of his art, he will fight on and he will continue to compose.

In fact, from this day, Beethoven will create some of the defining musical works of humanity. From the symmetry and clear logic of the classical age he will push the shape, the phrasing, the texture and the harmonic complexity of his music to places no-one else will dare to go for decades. From this day, Beethoven becomes the man whose music envelops the world and is the defining sound of our struggle between cruelty and joy.

Beethoven, in his art, supplies explanations to our deepest questions: not just why do we exist but how do we thrive?

Ludwig van Beethoven, Symphony No. 5 in C Minor
Is this the most famous beginning of them all? And why does Beethoven start with silence?

The classical symphony up to this point has been urbane and reasonable, more diplomatic than revolutionary. But in Beethoven's Fifth Symphony, the first three notes begin just after the actual start of the written bar. It's as if this sentence started with the word 'as', rather than 'it's'. In this music, the most defiant call to action of any in history, and where of the four opening notes, three of them are the same, Beethoven starts with an offbeat and we are caught off guard, our sword in its sheath on the settee, not in hand as with Joseph Bologne.

Perhaps Ludwig is feeling caught off guard as he composes this. The whole city, the whole country, is humiliated by Napoleon and his Grand Armée, who occupy Vienna at this point. Beethoven has already scratched out the dedication of his Third Symphony to Bonaparte with an action so enraged that he tears the paper. To think this man is now occupying Beethoven's beloved Vienna, it must make him galled beyond his gall bladder.

The music shoves its way into the crowd, the horns heckling from the sides, the centre's propulsion increased with the timpani and brass pushing, plunging into our brains. This music never gives in. It barges through our world, even that weird and wonderful oboe solo in the first movement, beguiling, persuading, ordering us to continue the good fight. We become Beethoven's soldiers with this music, obeying his command, struggling until the last note. Beethoven's Ninth Symphony is the one people refer to when we talk about hope, but this symphony is the sound of our crusade. We brawl, we scream, we counter, we purge. The Ninth is about an idea. The Fifth is pure action. Long live the struggle.

27

Picking a fight with Napoleon

Vienna, 8 April 1805. The morning after the premiere of Beethoven's Symphony No. 3, the *Eroica*. Reviews are out and they are, like a good cocktail, mixed. But unlike a good cocktail, the reviews do not improve Beethoven's mood.

One guy writes that the symphony is shrill and complicated, another that it is too long, another that it is completely disjointed. A symphony by Anton Eberl is played in the same concert and that is considered a better piece. Sorry, Anton who?

But how did we get here? Not that long ago, symphonies were lovely, neat affairs, with a couple of horns and some assorted woodwind and a running time of about twenty minutes, just enough to entertain you before you went outside for a pie and chips. Now Beethoven has written a symphony that lasts for three quarters of an hour, with not one, not two, but *three* horns to blast away at the back, and an approach to music that isn't exactly following the rules (which we learned just recently) of so-called classical music. His tunes are unpredictable, his harmonies leap wildly from one landscape to the next, and the dynamics — the louds and softs — are volatile and frequently ferocious.

All this riotous music might have something to do with a guy called Napoleon. Bonaparte, that is. Napoleon has picked fights with just about everyone in Europe and now he has gone and declared himself emperor. Beethoven started out liking Napoleon and dedicates his Third Symphony to him, but as soon as he finds out about the emperor declaration thing (Emperorgate?), he takes the score of this symphony, scratches out Napoleon's name with what appears to be a very sharp knife and exclaims that Napoleon will now be like all those other dodgy aristocrats who just tread the rights of humanity underfoot.

So we are in turbulent times and that calls for turbulent music. A style of composing called Sturm und Drang, storm and stress, has already hit the music stands, an art, literary and music style with dramatic changes of mood. Joseph Haydn uses the style in a few of his symphonies, and so do some of J.S. Bach's kids — C.P.E., J.C., W.F., P.D.Q., B.C.E. and L.O.L. ... (Oh okay, not the last three.) And, sad to say, it's an ideal style for war.

So here he is, Napoleon himself, listening to his favourite Italian vocal music by Giovanni Paisiello (it's tricky getting headphones over that bicorne hat), about to be defeated by the British and Lord Nelson in the Battle of Trafalgar (for which Haydn will compose his *Nelson Mass*), but then at the end of the year winning the Battle of Austerlitz against a Russo-Austrian army. Napoleon's wars are tearing apart Europe, inspiring Tolstoy to write *War and Peace* and making a real mess of music publishing. Now composers can only sell their rights to individual countries, which means the dissemination of music is curtailed for over a decade. War in music, as in everything, destroys collaboration and stunts healthy development.

But changes are afoot — no, a-ear — because the Romantics are putting on their fluffy shirts and bringing new sounds to the world. But perhaps the last words from the classical era should be from Napoleon: 'English music is vile, the worst in the world, and French music is almost as bad as the English. Italians are the only people who can produce an opera.' What would he think of Wagner?

Giovanni Paisiello, 'In My Heart I No More Feel the Sparkle of Youth'

So as not to annoy Napoleon any more than necessary, let's have a listen to some Paisiello.

Giovanni Paisiello is one of those composers whom you could so easily criticise for being an obsequious slimeball, but hey, who are we to judge? These people need to make money, right? The first dodgy thing Paisiello does is nick a storyline off the composer Giovani Battista Pergolesi and reset it; clearly karma does exist because with *The Barber of Seville*, Gioachino Rossini writes a much more successful version. Paisiello spreads a few bad stories around about other composers, moves to Russia and is eventually invited back to France by Napoleon himself, presumably after Napoleon has been hearing too much English music. As well as English tunes, Napoleon can't stand the music of Luigi Cherubini, so Paisiello badmouths him as well. You're getting the picture — Paisiello is one negative dude. His music, though, especially this aria, is fluffy chocolate-box-fluff-puff fluff itself. Perhaps not exactly memorable, but pleasing enough that Beethoven and Niccolò Paganini use it to compose some variations.

It all ends badly for Paisiello. He is shunned by the Parisians (so many of us are) and goes back to Italy with his wife, she dies suddenly and Paisiello doesn't last long after her. He leaves behind a curious mix of spiteful musings and delightful music. How perplexing.

28

Bel canto

You may have been thinking, as we go a bit further into the nineteenth century, that there hasn't been any word from opera recently. Sorry, any libretti from opera recently. Well, apart from the Paisiello.

Now that's a good point, so let's have a little recap and listen to what's been on, and off, the stage in the last few years.

You remember Jacopo Peri and the first opera, *Dafne*? After Peri comes a chorus of composers, most famously Claudio Monteverdi, who develops the solo song or aria, George Frideric Handel, who shines a bright light on the singers, and Christoph Willibald Gluck, who makes opera more about 'noble simplicity' and less about the vanity of those well-lit singers. Along the way, fewer operas are written about gods and more about your regular folk. Take Wolfgang Amadeus Mozart's *The Marriage of Figaro*, starring a servant, another servant and a duke who is bossed around by both the servants. There's Napoleon's favourite composer as well, Giovanni Paisiello, whose works influence

Mozart and who also has his opera idea called *The Barber of Seville* nicked, as we learned, by a bloke named Gioachino Rossini. Rossini becomes the most famous opera composer of the early 1800s, with some seriously catchy tunes, a simple style and very drawn-out crescendos. You remember that Mannheim rocket? Like that, but the Rossini rocket is heading to Mars, not just the moon.

Opera is now massive business. Opera houses are built throughout Europe, and in the 1800s, sitting in the best seats is equivalent to being an Instagram influencer and 'liked' by millions. But going to the opera is also about following your favourite singer, who is paid much more than the composer and certainly has only blue M&Ms in their dressing-room as per their rider. But those singers are changing. Someone noticed (crikey, they took their time) that castrating boys to preserve their lovely voices was perhaps a hard thing to sell, so women take on male roles (called a trouser role) and gradually the male tenor voice is given the role of lover and hero. The virtuosity of the baroque is refined into a beautiful, bel canto style, improvisation in arias is reduced and music is more completely written out.

But perhaps the most interesting thing in this operatic time happens not inside the opera theatre but outside it, because publishers take the famous bits from operas and put them all together into albums for the home singer and pianist. Now your auntie and uncle can combine to sing an aria from Rossini's *Tancredi*, jump to a little number from *Der Freischütz* by Carl Maria von Weber, then, after a spot of supper, have a bash at that latest hit from Bellini, all within the home! And it's not only a domestic song and dance. Operatic overtures make their way into concert programmes, opera highlights are performed at puppet shows and by barrel organists. This focus on the melody of opera and the split between the full work in the theatre and the highlights at home are some of the roots of musical theatre.

Now operas are bigger, the voices are louder, and next time we will look at how instruments are burgeoning too.

Gioachino Rossini, 'No Longer Sad', from *Cinderella*

Since this has been a chapter about opera, here's a bel canto song to finish from *Cinderella* by Gioachino Rossini. Yes, the servant has definitely turned into the princess.

Rossini has the type of career you might dream of — massive success in his twenties, fame, virtually nobody even close to his abilities as an opera composer, all the cake he can eat — then he retires in his thirties, moves to Paris, starts up a Saturday musical salon where Franz Liszt, Giuseppe Verdi and Richard Wagner come to visit, composes a few miniatures and that's it. Along the way he gains a reputation as a food-loving hedonist and composes some high-energy music — here is the party guy you were looking for. Although he retires at a trust-fund-kid kind of age, he is prolific till then, composing thirty-eight operas by the time he is thirty-eight himself. It's not all fun and games: Rossini loves to compose the arias, where he writes out all the ornamentation, but he dillies and dallies with the overtures and sometimes, writing literally at the last minute, throws the music sheets out of the window down to the copyist, who in turn sends them through to the orchestra, who are already rehearsing the

piece. If you are similarly tardy with your work, now you can quote Rossini as your inspiration.

Rossini's music is regarded as too populist by snooty critics, who make fun of him for not knowing all the rules of music. Rossini's reply to that is … to retire at thirty-eight.

Rossini is twenty-five when he composes *Cinderella*. Perhaps only a twenty-five-year-old could work at the speed he does: he completes the opera in three weeks, it becomes a success all over Europe and in New York and it's only as the skills of singers change that the opera is performed less. This final aria, 'No Longer Sad', is a gemstone of glittering music, virtuosic technique, playful tune and rhythmic development. Cinderella forgives her wicked stepfamily and spins us around with vocal gymnastics — coloratura (another word to impress your mum) is the fancy-pants technique the singers use here, and if you ever need to be reminded of the wide variety of abilities of humanity, listen to this aria. Especially with Cecilia Bartoli singing. We have come a long way from Gregorian chanting.

And what happens to Rossini? It's a lot of time to fill after retirement, as he lives until he is seventy-six. His extramarital affairs catch up with him and, with symptoms of gonorrhoea and some mental health issues, he moves back to Paris from Florence, regains his health and begins composing a few little pieces again. He calls these chamber and solo works *Sins of Old Age*. For Rossini, even his sins are our gift.

29

Higher, louder, faster

It's 1825 and here we are in the world's largest city, London.

The Congress of Vienna, that congress where everybody shook hands after waving ta-ta to Napoleon, who was finally and very permanently sent to an island, is celebrating its ten-year anniversary, and around the world it's Pax Britannica — peace, man, Pommie-style. The British are now the global kingpins, although that really should be queenpins, as Queen Victoria is sitting very firmly on her throne.

In a few years you will see horse-drawn omnibuses trot alongside balance bicycles and hear steam locomotives on elevated tracks. The world is moving faster and louder, but what does the development of transport, especially railways, have to do with music?

That is an excellent question, and here is a short answer: iron. As rail tracks are made stronger due to changes in iron production, iron is also used by piano makers to form frames for their pianos. And stronger frames means the tension on the strings can be higher, so there can be more strings per note and more notes (now we reach eighty-eight keys), which means the volume of the piano is becoming really LOUD. WHAT DID YOU SAY? The pitch of notes also rises by almost a semitone from baroque times.

Concert halls become bigger as demand for music grows, and now the modern orchestra is really taking shape: Mozart has already added clarinets; Beethoven trombones; we have trumpets and horns with valves that allow for a greater range of notes; oboes and clarinets have become higher and louder and easier to play quickly with new keys and bore size (just like your uncle at Christmas); for string instruments there have been dramatic changes in the bow (Niccolò Paganini, the violin virtuoso who could make his violin sound like a human crying or a farmyard animal, even tries out bows made from steel and proclaims them superior to wood); and now there are so many players they need a person to stand up at the front and wave a stick at them to keep them all together. This is the beginning of the culture of the maestro, the charismatic demigod figure of the conductor/composer.

Previously the bows for string instruments were, well, bowed outwards, but now two bow makers, or archetiers, John Dodd in London and François Tourte in Paris, independently of each other develop a way of steaming wood to bring more spring and tension to an inwardly sprung bow. This means that your violin or viola or cello or bass sound, which has already been changed by tilting the neck back to create a greater string tension, will now reach the last row of the biggest concert hall. And the string players can play with a smoother, more even sound from end to end of their bow, something that matches the bel canto of opera singers.

The wood the archetiers use is pernambuco, only grown in Brazil and obtained by the Englishman John Dodd from a curious source: barrels of rum. Look carefully at his bows today and you can still see the original holes for nails from the barrels, and if you take a very deep breath, you can still smell the faintest whiff of rum. Just kidding. Not about the nails though.

And in the next chapter, from the wall of sound of the orchestra to the intimacy of song, Schubert-style.

Fanny Mendelssohn, Piano Trio in D Minor
Felix Mendelssohn, 'The Hebrides'

The Mendelssohn family is the 1800s version of the Kanneh-Masons — prolific, brilliant, humble and with apparently endless ability. Fanny is a pianist, singer and composer, and she is considered by the siblings' composition teacher to be the more talented of the two. This seems like it might be the Nannerl Mozart situation all over again (the age difference between the pairs of siblings is the same), but it's not quite that bad. Still, it's also not that good. Her family merely puts up with her musical achievements instead of giving her the outright support they give Felix. Oh gosh, don't you just want to scream at this? Fanny says about her own composing that she does not have the skills to sustain development of themes in a big work and so she prefers to compose shorter pieces, like songs. But what songs! Fanny has a kaleidoscopic sense of variety, a popular ability with melody and her rhythms are hypnotic. Felix advises his sister to not publish her music under her own name but apparently thinks it's good enough to publish under his. What sort of brother does that? Queen Victoria, on meeting Felix, raves about her favourite song, which she thinks is composed by Felix; at least he isn't a complete **** and does admit his sister wrote it. A bit different from Samuel Dushkin and Maria Theresia von Paradis.

Fanny and Felix both compose a piano trio in D minor: Felix's is played and celebrated in his lifetime; Fanny's is only published after her death. What people have missed out on. Fanny becomes friends with Clara Schumann (more about this superwoman in a couple of chapters) and sees a lot of Clara as she creates this piece, just months before her death. This is music with grand horizons, intimate nooks, a sonic system of feeling and, yes, development of themes to match and surpass her brother.

Back in 1830, while Fanny is stuck at home giving birth to her son, Felix is swanning around Europe on his Grand Tour and ends up in Scotland. He has a disastrous meeting with Sir Walter Scott, who is on his way out the door of his castle when Felix and his mate show up, so it's not surprising that Sir Walter isn't that welcoming. Felix is inspired by Scotland, though, and composes his Scottish Symphony and the overture 'The Hebrides', or 'Fingal's Cave'. Felix visits the Isle of Staffa and is overawed by the sounds and smells of the cave, especially of the oil, the dead fish and the seagulls. It's true, in Scotland the seagulls are the size of pterodactyls, and the cave is literally awesome and fishy beyond fishiness.

This overture is one of the first in a new style — a concert overture. As you may remember, an overture is literally an opening to something, usually an opera or a ballet, but now Felix writes a piece which is its own world, with a beginning and an end, a musical island about an island. With the wall of sound that is developing in this time, Felix harnesses the power of the orchestra as if it is the sea and swell itself. The walls of the cave, with their hexagonal basalt columns linked in legend to the Giant's Causeway in Northern Ireland, become walls of music, a giant's causeway leading to now.

Fanny and Felix, always close in life, are also close in death. Fanny dies first, at the age of forty-one, from a stroke as she rehearses some of her brother's music. Felix dies months later, also of a stroke. He is thirty-eight years old.

30

Take me to your lieder

Vienna, 21 November 1828. Franz Schubert will be buried today, only a year after he was a pallbearer at Beethoven's funeral. Schubert leaves behind a thousand works, a figure hard to comprehend when he lived for a mere thirty-one years.

Among Schubert's works are sonatas, symphonies, quartets, overtures and six hundred songs, or lieder.

But why did Schubert compose so many songs?

You will remember the 1815 Congress of Vienna and all those changes in society and technology. Add to that the development of music printing with lithography, which now means publishers can print and sell music for lower prices, which creates a bigger market, which leads to more demand, which means composers are paid more to write more, which also means, as the market is buoyant, composers can now experiment. No more being careful and sticking to the classical style with its elegance and, let's admit it, a sometimes trite predictability. Composers are no longer beholden to royalty or aristocracy or the church, since they are now freelancers, and the more experimental their music, the better it sells.

Schubert, like Beethoven before him, walks further and further from the classical style and more and more towards the new Romantic philosophy: the expression of the self, individuality, with a celebration of solitude and independence. This is shown in music with more extreme harmonies, evoking the emotion of poetry through the piano accompaniment. Now composers are wondering, with an 'o', and wandering, with an 'a', as lonely as a cloud and making songs of intense love, searching for identity and with profound acknowledgement of the inevitability of death.

So how better to portray all these intense emotions than with the lied. You can take a strophic poem, change the background of the piano every verse so there is even more of a feeling of story, then put the song into a group with other poems by the same poet and, hey presto, you have yourself a song cycle to go with that new balance cycle you've got in the garage. Beethoven is the first to write a song cycle with his 'An die Ferne Geliebte', and by the time you get to Schubert, in 1815 alone he composes 140 songs.

The opening to 'Gretchen am spinnrade', or 'Gretchen at the Spinning Wheel', is machinery as music. Schubert writes this just before his eighteenth birthday. You can hear with the piano accompaniment the sound of the spinning wheel going round and round and round, a feeling of eternity in just a few notes, with a new harmonic daring and bigger, stranger steps between chords.

Robert Schumann, the German composer, carries the baton after Schubert and has his own year of song — 120 songs in 1840. Schumann is desperate to marry Clara Wieck, and you can feel the kiss of his music in his 'Dichterliebe', or 'A Poet's Love', a song cycle of poems by Heinrich Heine. The drama from the cycle — especially the song 'Ich grolle nicht', 'I Do Not Complain' — seems to sum up Robert's life at the time; after all, he is suing Clara's dad to be able to marry her.

But if anyone should be complaining it's Clara Weick. She does marry Schumann eventually, but as you'll find out in the next chapter, things don't exactly go to plan …

Franz Schubert, *Winter Journey*

Is there anything as sad as travelling on your own through a winter's landscape, shut out of love, shut out in the cold? It's a despicable feeling, and Franz, this dear young man who barely has a chance to grow up, somehow catches this individual, universal tragedy in just a few chords. A pulsing, a sigh, a chilling tread of death. After Johann Sebastian Bach, Franz Schubert is the man who can transport us out of this dimension to one of the purest vibrations. With Schubert, even our death is a gladdening.

His song cycle *Die Winterreise* is a setting of poems by Wilhem Müller for voice and piano. Here is a work of art where its authors, Schubert and Müller, not only lay bare their hearts but also show such enormous compassion for the suffering of our world. Schubert uses the briefest of gestures, tiny little phrases which he abuses over and over, almost tortuous in their repetition. Schubert is the one of the roots of minimalism, a musician of few notes. No, a musician of the perfect number of notes.

A word of warning: this is not a song cycle to listen to if you're feeling depressed. As the title suggests, the author wanders through an infinitely frigid landscape, trying to find love and warmth. He never does.

31

Clara Schumann, superwoman

So far we have been for special walks with only two composers, Johann Sebastian Bach and Ludwig van Beethoven. But here we are in February 1854 in Dusseldorf and, unfortunately, due to time and work constraints, the following composer has declined the invitation of a walk but has agreed to an interview, if she can stay at home and look after her kids as well. So here we are, at the Schumanns' house ...

Clara: Yes, hello, how can I help you? Ludwig! Stop that. Please go back inside ...
ELB: Ah, hello, Frau Wieck, I mean, Schumann? Sorry. My name's Ed Le Brocq — I wrote to you about going for a walk and an interview but I realise you're very busy. You mentioned that I could come round and talk with you if I didn't mind your kids being around as well and ... is now a good time?
Child: Mama! Mama!

Clara: Well, I am very busy today. Ludwig, I told you before, please put your sister down. Yes, but on her feet, not her head … Look, my husband is not very well at all, I need to take him to the hospital this afternoon. And the children have got to do their lessons and they are already upset about their daddy leaving. So I'm not sure I have a lot of time, but come on, let's just make it really quick, okay?

ELB: Wonderful, thank you so much!

Clara: Alright, come this way, don't mind the mess. The children are very untidy, but we have to cherish them, don't we? Who knows how long any of us will live …

ELB: Yes, Frau Schumann, I'm so sorry to hear about your son Emil …

Clara: Well, thank you. Yes, he was just a year old, we don't even know why he died. We've only got seven children now; I hope they are going to stay upstairs this morning … Now, how can I help you?

ELB: Well, I'm from the future, and in most countries, women's rights and education are generally better than in your time, but I'd love to know about your own concert career and the challenges you have faced.

Clara: Well, I think the biggest challenge right now is to stop my children from killing each other. Marie, please don't do that to your sister. Noses are for breathing, not sticks … Sorry … yes, my career, well, my mum started teaching me the piano when I was four, and when she left my dad took over. He was very strict — I practised for two hours every day at least. I don't remember much playtime, but you know, it worked out because I gave my debut when I was nine. Then I met Robert, my husband, well, my future husband at the time.

ELB: Now I know you had to reduce your concertising for a few years after you married Robert, but what do you think is going to happen now?

Clara: Yes, well, you know when you're a wife in the 1800s, you have to, er, bow down to your husband a little, but the fact is that Robert and I would travel around Europe and I was the famous one! I don't think he liked that very much. But we have met some wonderful people! I loved spending time with Fanny Mendelssohn, and young Brahms is a favourite — everyone thinks we are romantically involved but it's just not true. Now Robert is going into hospital I'll need to go back to work and play a few more concerts. I think I'm going to England next year or so, but you know the English, they are terrible with their short rehearsal times. I mean, how can you make my music beautiful if you just run through it once?

ELB: Frau Schumann, I'm sorry to say that English rehearsals are not any longer in the twenty-first century. One more question, if you've got time: what advice would you give composers today, particularly female composers?

Clara: Well, first of all, don't let your father dictate whom you marry! Robert and I had to take my dad to court to let us marry. And secondly, never give up your career for your husband. Their egos can survive a successful wife, and if not, you've married the wrong man. Now I'm sorry, you'll have to excuse me — I have to get Robert to hospital, and these children ... Stop that, Elise! You know, I had to walk through an uprising to rescue these kids a few years ago, and now I have an uprising in my own home. Thanks for coming, and I wondered ... do you still listen to my music where you come from?

ELB: Frau Schumann, you'll be pleased to know that we listen to your music as much as we listen to your husband's.

Clara: Oh goody! But please, one tiny request. Don't tell Robert.

Clara Schumann, Piano Concerto in A Minor

All music is energised, motivated, by passion. It can be a passion of money, fame, jealousy, experimentation, freedom, hatred, knowledge, revolution or love. Clara Schumann composes what will become the final movement of this concerto when she is thirteen but it is put on hold for a while until love comes into her life. A motivation. A passion. Clara is fifteen years old when she falls in love, not with Robert Schumann but with a cellist called August Theodor Müller, and it is this cellist, this love, that motivates Clara to compose the second movement of her piano concerto. 'The Romance' (the title is a giveaway) is a love song between the solo piano and a solo cello, a line of music taking us on a glorious ridge of song. The moment when the cello enters, after a long eulogy from the piano, is one of the great releases in music. This is a sound to overcome an arid place, a virtual pas de deux, with the rest of the orchestra merely spectators to a love scene. There has been a worrying number of people in music education in more recent times who believe music by female composers is not equal to the men of their time, that their music is not worth including in textbooks or examinations. Clara takes these small-minded men and stuffs their ears with music so well-sculpted that Rodin himself is wondering how he can do better. Perhaps the reason so many people (mostly male critics) thought for so long that Clara's music wasn't as 'good' as male composers is because she has a diaphanous liberty, something few men can match.

Clara will complete the first movement of the concerto just before her sixteenth birthday and give its premiere with Felix

Mendelssohn conducting. You can only hope Clara's good friend Fanny is in the audience.

Clara is truly the superwoman of music — she gives thousands of concert performances, her playing is admired by her fellow musicians and the critics of her time, she gives birth to eight children whom she eventually looks after on her own, four of them pre-decease her, her husband and oldest son are dragged off to mental institutions and she goes deaf towards the end of her life. She will be one of the leaders in the War of the Romantics (more in a couple of chapters) and is not only a guiding light for women but for all. Clara dies from a stroke just after playing music by one of the great loves of her life, Johannes Brahms.

32

Notes that build the nation

You may remember from a few chapters and several hundred years ago that in the sixteenth and seventeenth centuries, music had begun to have clearer distinctions in different countries. Then things got a bit smudged together in the later 1700s, but now in 1848, the times, as someone called Bob sings, they are a changing.

The year 1848 is massive. Yes, MASSIVE. It's not called the Springtime of Nations for nuthin'. Liberia swears in its first president; Karl Marx and Friedrich Engels publish their *Communist Manifesto*; rebellion and revolution breaks out in France, Hungary, Sri Lanka, Poland and various states in soon-to-be Italy; Switzerland becomes a democratic republic; Ireland and other countries suffer the devastating effects of the Great Famine; and among all this, the song 'Simple Gifts' is composed in Maine by Joseph Brackett.

But what does this mean for music? Well, perhaps the strongest way a country can help forge its identity is through music, particularly its folk song and dance. So in the mid-1800s we hear Polish dances, mazurkas and polonaises transformed into musical jewels by Chopin; we hear Berlioz turning the German influences of strict form and development on their well-groomed heads with his *Symphonie Fantastique*; we hear Verdi in Italy summon the crowds with his epic operas of Italian unity, especially in *Nabucco*; in Germany we hear Carl Maria von Weber and his nationalist opera *Der Freischutz* (The Freeshooter), performed in defiance of years of occupation by Napoleonic forces; in Spain we hear Isaac Albeniz and his distillation of Spanish flavour, 'Iberia'; in Wales we hear Welsh songs composed by Joseph Parry; in the emerging Czech Republic we see Bedřich Smetana compose his epic ode to place, 'Ma Vlast (My Country)'; and that's soon to be followed by Antonín Dvořák and his use of Moravian folk song.

A little later on, Edvard Grieg's music in Norway will help shape their national identity, and for Jean Sibelius, it's hard to imagine Finland without the sound of 'Finlandia'.

People are fighting for the right to control their own lives, not have a strange, distant power tell them what to do, and this sound of nationalism is also heard intensely in Russia, with Mikhail Glinka and his new sonic image of his homeland. Glinka inspires five composers — Mily Balakirev, César Cui, Modest Mussorgsky, Nikolai Rimsky-Korsakov and Alexander Borodin — who collectively became known as the Mighty Handful or the Russian Five, and whose music will define the Russian sound world until Soviet times.

People who seek influence know the power of a good song. Just think of politicians walking onstage at a conference. If the song doesn't fit, their ratings slump. The mid-1800s in music are ratings heaven for nations. Now, with just a rhythm, a chord, an accent, people are hearing their own language in their own music, and it's changing the world.

Giuseppe Verdi, 'Chorus of the Hebrew Slaves', from *Nabucco*

You know you've won the hearts of people when they put down hay on the streets to cushion the sound of horses as you lie dying. That is a sign of love. And it's because Giuseppe Verdi has given Italy their clarion cry, 'Va, pensiero'.

With this chorus, which describes the love of the enslaved Jewish people for their homeland, Verdi gives a musical union to his country folk as they try to take their land from Austrian control. It's not only a musical refuge — this chorus becomes an inspiration for the Risorgimento, the unification of Italy.

We are lucky this opera is written at all. Verdi has just lost his wife and children to disease, his first opera, a comedy, is a bigger belly flop than a blue whale at the local swimming pool and Verdi is determined to give up composing. One day a friend throws Verdi a libretto to read that falls open on the 'Va, pensiero' page and that's it. Twenty-eight operas later, at the age of eighty-seven, Verdi lies dying in the Grand Hotel et de Milan, with the public insisting on almost hourly health updates. Here in Australia, this level of love is reserved for national icons like Richard Gill. 'Va, pensiero' is sung at Verdi's funeral.

As well as the words, the beauty of this chorus is in its unison singing, with the octaves of the men and women creating a bond of song, a metaphor for unification with a faint shadow of chant. It's not surprising that there is a proposal for the chorus to be made Italy's national anthem.

Verdi is still a hugely popular composer, two hundred years after his birth. He expands the size of the opera orchestra, makes it more muscular and composes idiosyncratically for each instrument. He concentrates everything on the success of the drama of the work and creates imaginary worlds to match Charles Dickens and his novels.

As music starts to split in the War of the Romantics (Richard Wagner, born in the same year as Verdi, is one side of the war), Verdi is criticised by some for not being traditional enough, but who cares? The glory of Verdi is that he writes such easy and, yes, catchy melodies, and he bathes them in glory with his harmonies. Verdi is just right. Verdi is al dente.

33

Tchaikovsky

The north bank of the Moscow River, 1882. In a tent next to the nearly completed Cathedral of Christ the Saviour (a cathedral that will eventually be torn down by the Soviets and rebuilt by the Russian Federation) comes a sound never heard before from a symphony orchestra concert — the sound of cannon fire. The *1812 Overture*, written to immortalise the defeat of Napoleon's army by the Russians, is coming to the climax in its premiere performance. And with it, the success of Pyotr Ilyich Tchaikovsky is assured.

But is it?

In the previous chapter we talked about nationalism in music and that idea of a sound helping to define a country's view of itself. In Russia, five composers come to dominate the national sound. This Russian Five, or the Mighty Handful, are using Russian folk song, harmony and rhythm, and they have turned away from a more European sound. But for Tchaikovsky, that isn't how he wants to compose. He needs musical freedom, all the freedom of harmony, rhythm and form to convey a new type of music, the beginnings of an exploration into the psychology of humanity.

During his life, Tchaikovsky is frequently torn between worlds: between Russia and Europe, between strict society and his illegal homosexuality, between craving intimacy and never meeting his patron, Nadezhda von Meck, between sacred and secular, between seeking critical approval and writing melodies whistled by the masses. What would we feel if we met Tchaikovsky today? Might we feel his confusion? His despair? After all, he writes this: 'I have found nothing — neither religion nor philosophy, to ease my troubled soul. But I would go mad were it not for music. Music is heaven's best gift to humanity. It alone clarifies, reconciles and consoles.'

Tchaikovsky will only live to the age of fifty-three, yet he writes hundreds of pieces: ten operas, six symphonies, solo piano pieces for the amateur market, sacred music for the Orthodox church, epic concertos still considered to be the epitome of the form, symphonic works like the *1812 Overture*, *Romeo and Juliet* and *Francesca Da Rimini* and three ballets. Oh, those ballets. *Swan Lake*, *The Nutcracker*, *Sleeping Beauty* ... Their tunes come to

signify the Romantic age. Tchaikovsky's style is brightly coloured, with complex textures and a natural feel for repetition where the listener can take time to hear a tune over and over again yet never become bored, because Tchaikovsky creates such sublime melody.

With the constant struggle in Tchaikovsky's life, both inner and outer, it is somehow not surprising that his death is surrounded by mystery. He drinks a glass of unboiled water during a cholera epidemic. Why? Was he being blackmailed over his homosexual affairs? Was he already ill? We will probably never know. Tchaikovsky's music takes the best of all worlds and, perhaps more than any other, propels despair and joy into our hearts in equal measure.

Pyotr Ilyich Tchaikovsky, Serenade for Strings

It is tempting to wallow a little in Tchaikovsky's music, either in the honey of his ballets or the turmoil of his symphonies, so perhaps it's time to take a rest and simply sit in the sunshine of this serenade.

Tchaikovsky travels abroad for about a year in the late 1870s, escaping and recovering from a disastrous marriage to one of his students, Antonina Miliukova. Tchaikovsky is gay and marries Antonina to arrest rumours; she wants to have sex with him, and as you can imagine if you are pressed in such a situation, he goes into mental breakdown and his brother takes him away. Antonina lives a long, sad life; she dies in 1917 and her last twenty years are spent in a mental institution.

Tchaikovsky creates this piece very quickly in Ukraine in the summery autumn of 1880, and he is welcomed home to the Moscow Conservatory by the students and professors performing this for him as a surprise. Tchaikovsky's heart must be so glad during this time to be successful, to be free of heterosexual demands, to be free to simply write music. Not even the slow movement in this serenade is glum. Every note has a slant of the sun in it, every note is unfettered, and this piece leads the way for other joyful string serenades to come, by Antonín Dvořák, Josef Suk and Edward Elgar. He gives a nod to the past, with references to Mozart and Russian folk songs, but also nods to the present with the inclusion of that shocking dance, the waltz, where you hold a partner so close that you can whisper things in their ear. With this piece, Tchaikovsky seems to be saying, 'I just don't care what you think of me.' Perhaps, in its freedom, this is his coming-out party.

34

European music bifurcation championship

Bifurcate (intransitive verb): to split into two branches.

'Bifurcate' is a word usually associated with roads, so when you hear it used with music you may feel a little bifurcated yourself. However, in the latter part of the nineteenth century, music really does bifurcate in something called the War of the Romantics. Admittedly, this does sound like Simon Le Bon and David Bowie rowing over who is wearing the best eye makeup (Bowie, obviously). To illustrate this shocking musical affair, we would like to present to you the European Music Bifurcation Championship, otherwise known as a slanging match.

Don't worry, the contestants are wearing full protection. Well, not Richard Wagner — we tried but he declined. Said he was a big toughie, or something like that.

BRAHMS

And in the blue corner, Johannes Brahms! Brahms is wearing his favourite sporty velvet tuxedo tonight and having a last smoke of one of his famous cigars. Holding his towel but hopefully not throwing it in just yet is Brahms's best buddy, Clara Schumann. The blue corner medic tonight is critic Eduard Hanslick, who is viciously critical of Wagner and his long, one might say endless, operas; we are going to have to make sure Hanslick stays outside the ropes. Clara is giving Brahms a last-minute pep talk: music for music's sake, the relationship of major and minor is paramount, none of those experimental chords or harmonies, and do not, not, *not* let your guard down while defending your symphony! Music does not need a story to be valid. And keep it short!

And in the red corner, Richard Wagner! Wagner's sitting on a giant ring-shaped stool that doesn't look very comfortable, and is

WAGNER

wearing a rather dramatic Teutonic knight costume, sword and all; someone's going to have to tell him he can't use that in the fight, only musical instruments are allowed tonight. Wagner's second is the pianist Franz Liszt — an excellent choice, he does compose some very experimental music with a lot of notes — and the medic is Cosima Liszt, Franz's daughter and Wagner's second wife. Liszt is giving a very speedy pep talk — crikey, there are so many words: no more symphonies, music needs a story, let's lose the boring old sense of key and home notes, forget about balance of phrasing, and above all, keep the fight going and do not, not, *not* stop before four hours are up!

And the surprise referee for tonight is conductor Hans von Bülow — not sure about that choice given he used to be married to Cosima before she ditched him for Wagner. Time will tell.

And the bell is ringing: round one!

Brahms has come out into the ring, he's still smoking his cigar. Someone should tell him smoking is bad for you. Bit of a heavyweight Brahms, his hook can be devastating, but Wagner is circling — he's ditched the sword but is now holding a Wagner tuba, his own invention! He's brandishing it above his head … no, he's blowing into it and making a very loud noise. Brahms is fighting back but all he's got is a cello, it's no match for the Wagner tuba; he's trying to pull a grand piano into the ring but the ref is refusing, it's disallowed. Clara Schumann has got up to put in a protest and is climbing into the ring now with a couple of flutes. Wagner has taken advantage of the distraction and brought in twenty brass players — there's no stopping them, they're playing the final sixteen hours of Wagner's *Ring* cycle condensed into a minute, the noise is deafening. Brahms crumples to the floor holding his ears. It looks like the game is up.

Von Bülow is going over to Brahms, counting him out in waltz time, one-two-three, one-two-three, and that's it! The ref takes Brahms's cigar out of his mouth and hands it over to Wagner. Brahms is down and he is definitely out.

All over in one round! Wagner didn't even have to go the length of his shortest opera, which is four hours. Over in the blink of a horn call and the upstarts have it! And now the brass are playing a funeral march. It sounds like Siegfried's 'Funeral March' from the *Ring* … Oh dear, this is a tough blow for Brahms and we may have to wait maybe a century until his music makes a proper comeback. Until then, Brahms is finished with and it's Wagner, with all his new harmonies, his new instruments (why hello again, Wagner tuba), his narrative music and his very, *very* long operas, who is the European champion.

Note from editor: No musicians or instruments were hurt in the making of this chapter.

Richard Wagner, 'Siegfried Idyll'

The rest of this book could be taken up by Wagner's *Ring* cycle (yes, the whole thing really does last about sixteen hours), but let's instead stick with one of our champ Wagner's more pithy works, the 'Siegfried Idyll'. Coming in at around twenty minutes (depending on the ego of the conductor), this is a veritable musical ditty.

Now picture this: Christmas Day, 1870, a villa on the shore of Lake Lucerne, the snow falling outside, the Alps in the distance. You are woken by string players sinking into a pillow of melody and you wander out onto the landing. There, arrayed down the staircase, are thirteen musicians playing you a love song. The big question is, will they want breakfast afterwards? Oh dear, there's only enough pop tarts for two.

Look, if you don't like Wagner (hmm, does the 'Ride of the Valkyries' count?), you just might like this. Give it a go at least. Wagner's music can be endless, confusing, ridiculous, life-changing and thrilling; this short work, written for his wife Cosima's birthday, is the very best of Wagner: luscious tunes, clever arranging of the music between the instruments (called orchestration), a clear journey through time and space and emotion, a satisfying ending, and enough repetition that you will come away humming the main tune.

Even Wagner can write a pop song.

This is a short chapter. Wagner, please take note.

35

A New World order

Just before we wave a final lace-gloved goodbye to the nineteenth century, we need to pop into another country. Not just another country, another continent — North America, and specifically the United States.

Music in the United States has been influenced throughout the 1800s by immigrants from all over the world, and many of those immigrants have come from a country where music is potent and important: Germany. Classical composers such as Amy Beach and Edward MacDowell are influenced by Brahms or Wagner, although their music doesn't quite capture the heart of Americans as more popular styles do.

A short history of Western classical music really wouldn't be complete without a quote from Liberace, would it? Here is the glittering man introducing one of his TV specials: 'I'm happy to be with all of you again. And our programme today is dedicated to the music and the life of one of America's greatest composers, Stephen Foster. And to start off the programme, here is one of his very exciting and rollicking tunes, "Camptown Races".' Cue sparkles.

This first truly popular American composer (he'd have to be to make it onto Liberace's show) has British roots. Stephen Foster takes the art song style of Europe and brings it to the American parlour, with songs like 'Camptown Races' and 'Oh! Susanna'; these melodies and sound celebrations become the scaffolding of the country's emerging identity. Foster dies at the age of thirty-seven from a fever (with possible evidence of suicidal intent), towards the end of the American Civil War. This war is described as the most musical in history, which sounds strange, but just as music was crucial for the opposing sides in the French Revolution, the same has happened in the New World, with virtually every regiment having a band to entertain, inspire and perform during battle. Crikey, you'd want to choose your performance spot carefully. That hilltop isn't looking so attractive. After the war, the surviving musicians play in community bands and, with cheaper and easier-to-play instruments, these bands grow and grow until many of them turn professional. There are enormous band festivals with tens of thousands of performers, and people like 'Waltz King' Johann Strauss Jr turn up from Vienna to conduct.

But nobody does band like the newly crowned 'March King' John Philip Sousa. His marches, well, they march on endlessly: 'Liberty Bell', 'The Washington Post', 'The Stars and Stripes Forever'. These tunes go straight to the ear and the heart, and that's what people want. As the nineteenth century reaches its end, popular songs, with their emphasis on an easily sung motif or hook, make their creators rich. Many of these composers and their publishers work in the Tin Pan Alley neighbourhood in New York City; they pump out the tunes and the public buy the sheet music. In their millions.

But perhaps the most influential of all these immigrants are the people who never asked to come, African-Americans who were enslaved, others murdered, and yet their culture and music will become the root of so much. White people try to crush their spirits in every way and yet their act of singing survives, with rhythms, syncopations, forms and melodies from many different parts of Africa. African-American spirituals are heard in society in many different ways — as folk music, as popular songs sung at home, and as source material for classical composers.

Syncopation, a rhythm where the main beat is missed so the tune becomes offbeat, is the kernel of ragtime. Ragtime begins with players improvising on straight tunes, and just before the twentieth century these rhythms are notated fully, just as Gioacchino Rossini does with his coloratura arias. Understandably, people go wild for it. Scott Joplin, the son of a former slave, is the most famous of these ragtime composers, yet he has to fight so much prejudice. He composes two operas and even a book of studies for this new style, a ragtime primer, but still many people deny the music any standing. Racism is in people's ears and hearts. In the United States, classical music, popular music and folk music are drifting further and further apart, and ragtime, some of the most popular music of all, is about to morph into another great style — jazz.

Scott Joplin, 'A Real Slow Drag', from *Treemonisha*

Scott Joplin is one of those people who, when you read about their life and challenges, you want to cheer and cry and scream from the future, wishing it could have been different, but applauding how bloody courageous and resilient they are.

Joplin is born in Texas (no-one is sure where) around the year 1868 (no-one is sure when) and is the son of a freeborn African-American woman and a former slave. He goes to college, plays in his own band at the Chicago world fair, sets up his own piano studio and eventually strikes up a business relationship with a publisher, with whom he signs a contract for one cent per sale of his 'Maple Leaf Rag'. One cent doesn't sound like much, but when the sales go into the millions it becomes a nice little earner for Joplin for the rest of his life.

Joplin becomes the proclaimed, and self-proclaimed, 'King of Ragtime' as this style of music becomes massive in the US. Joplin is the Guillaume de Machaut of the fin de siècle, despite losing his child and his second wife ten weeks into their marriage.

Treemonisha is Joplin's third stage work. The main character is Treemonisha, an educated woman who is abducted by conjurors who eventually release her, realising how important education is both for men and women. With this opera, Joplin synthesises the rhythms and phrases of African-American music with the harmonies and forms of Western classical music.

In 'A Real Slow Drag', the final piece in the opera, you can hear the beginnings of the sounds of Kurt Weill and cabaret — the snarl, the sarcasm. And the speed matches Joplin's own instruction for his music: 'It is never right to play ragtime fast.'

The blues will receive similar instruction, to be played as slowly as 'an old man dragging his feet through the cotton plants'.

As syphilis continues its invasion of his brain, Joplin is desperate to make *Treemonisha* a success. He publishes a vocal and piano score at his own expense and puts on a performance for potential investors. It is a disaster, many walk out, and Joplin experiences a complete breakdown, is institutionalised and dies a year later in 1917 at the age of forty-eight. He is buried in an unmarked grave, his achievements and grave only fully recognised after the awarding of a Pulitzer Prize in 1976.

36

The cowbell and the concert hall

Question: How does a cowbell make it to a concert hall?
Answer: Well, you could say it's because the cow's horns don't
work, but it has more to do with a man called Gustav Mahler,
and specifically his childhood.

The year is 1889 and Mahler's first symphony has just premiered
in Budapest to not exactly glowing praise. From one critic: 'a
considerable part of the audience, in its usual heartless way,
had no understanding of anything formally new ... they were
uncomfortably startled out of their thoughtless habit.' Ouch.
Mahler himself writes: 'In Pest, where I performed it for the
first time, my friends bashfully avoided me afterward; nobody
dared talk to me about the performance and my work, and I
went around like a sick person or an outcast.'

But what is the problem? Well, just like the cowbells, the
answer comes from Mahler's childhood.

Mahler is born into a Jewish family, speaking German in Czech lands. On top of Mahler's feeling of exclusion for speaking German and being Jewish in a mostly Christian society, his parents also fight bitterly, with his dad using physical violence against his mum. In a meeting with Sigmund Freud, Mahler describes the perennial antithesis of his life, violence shoved against playfulness — when he is a child, Mahler runs out of the house as his parents are arguing viciously inside, and right there outside an organ grinder is playing a cheerful popular song.

And with this scene, music of the late nineteenth century begins a deep psychological self-analysis, a synthesis of folk and international style. Mahler steps into the symphonic world with his first symphony in as surprising a way as Beethoven did, not even a hundred years before. Mahler brings a sound as if from within his own ear, a tinnitus-high pitch from the violins underpinned by seven octaves of instruments, making a profound sonic pillar. No wonder people are confused. Where is the tune? And as a distant cry, military-sounding trumpets play from beyond the stage, from beyond consciousness. It really is now that psychology and music combine. What is happening?

Mahler takes this disturbing beginning and turns it on its head by quoting his own song, 'I Went Over the Field This Morning', from his cycle *Songs of a Wayfarer*. When he is criticised for repeating and quoting himself, he simply says, 'Composing is like playing with bricks, continually making new buildings from the same old stones.' And after all, how many times will Monet paint his lilies? (With this statement, you do wonder why Mahler isn't more appreciative of Arnold

Schoenberg, of twelve-tone method fame, although Mahler is kind enough to pay Arnold's rent for a year.)

So already, in the first few minutes of the work, we have a brave new world: a penetrating stillness, a riot of off-stage violence, then a sublime melody from a completely different planet. And that's just the beginning. Mahler will go on to expand the numbers of players both on stage and off, he will develop programmatic works and then hide their meaning (in the style of Hector Berlioz), he will begin to dissolve the strict relationship between major and minor, he will vary the texture so that in one moment you are hearing the full orchestra of now more than a hundred players and then, in a single note of vertigo, change to a solo violin and clarinet. And yes, he brings in that humble cowbell from his childhood, a sound he describes as 'the last greeting from earth to penetrate the remote solitude of the mountain peaks'.

In short, Mahler is telling us that there is nothing we can rely on, nothing can be certain, everything is a mere note away from calamity or bliss. Here is a musical prelude to Franz Kafka's *The Metamorphosis*.

Mahler's music is dragging us into the twentieth century. And it is a portent of the unbounded destruction to come.

Gustav Mahler, Symphony No. 6 in A Minor

Music and superstition, music and myth, music and death, music and premonition — this is the symphony that has it all. And a Mahler hammer as well.

By the time Mahler composes this symphony in 1903–04, he

has persuaded Alma Schindler to marry him, despite making her surrender her own music career to be at his beck and call. As you listen to this symphony, think of Alma, who tells Gustav to get stuffed, leaves him for the architect Walter Gropius and during the Second World War escapes with her third husband, the writer Franz Werfel, over the Pyrenees, makes her way to New York and becomes a cultural idol. Gustav, what were you thinking?

But what has changed with this symphony from Beethoven's time? First of all, the size of the orchestra — extra everybody, with extended woodwinds and brass, eight horns, a comprehensive percussion section that includes offstage cowbells (is that because they still have the cow attached?), a celesta, six timpani (in Haydn's time there were only two), and two harps. The length of the symphony has also swollen from around thirty minutes for an early Beethoven symphony to thirty minutes for the last movement alone of the Mahler. The whole thing can last nearly an hour and a half. This isn't a symphony — this is an intergalactic odyssey. One moment we are making our way through a brawl of brass players, the next we are ambling through an alpine meadow accompanied by bells and lush strings. In the first movement, Mahler uses an iconic form of the classical era, sonata form, and he uses the classical number of movements, four. Even though Mahler is pushing the boundaries, in his own way he is still very much painting within the frame. This music has so many layers, with snippets of melody that build and build, just as the skyscrapers are going up and up, and then … the void.

In a direction that has the musical intensity of an aural black hole, Mahler makes use of a sound never conceived before now: the hammer blow of fate. Mahler includes three hammer blows in the final movement, which have been interpreted as events in his life: the death of his daughter, his diagnosis of heart disease and the termination of his contract at the Vienna Court Opera. Mahler directs that the sound should be a 'short, powerful, heavy-sounding blow of non-metallic quality, like the stroke of an axe'. This can lead to some inventive solutions by the percussion section; one of the most effective (in a chilling, end-of-hope kind of way) is to use a plank of wood and smash it down to the concert platform. All energy is sucked into this instant.

Throughout the symphony, Mahler turns the lights on and then off again with a sudden change of chordal tonality from major to minor. After all that effort, all that development over time by Rameau, Bach, Beethoven and Wagner, this shift now has enormous significance. Now, it reveals to us the truth of life: there is always darkness because there is always light.

Alban Berg, genius composer himself, declares this the only symphony number six. Sorry, Beethoven.

37

Death and transfiguration

You know the score: you've been wearing the same old shirt for a while, eating the same old food, and it feels like you've been doing the same old thing for the last three hundred years. Well, when composers think about composing yet another symphony in the late nineteenth century, they often feel the same way. So you can understand why they might be a little … unenthusiastic.

The symphony is a form that started in the late 1600s as an orchestral intro to opera, and although by Mahler's time it is getting very long and very big, it's still a symphony. Sure, Beethoven does change things up with his Ninth Symphony, adding a chorus and solo singers, then Mahler does the same thing, just for longer. But stuff gotta change, otherwise it's a bit like rebranding Brussels sprouts — if you've been eating them a lot, even roasting them with garlic and thyme isn't going to work. You need something new. How about a Savoy cabbage?

And ta-da, it's time for the overture to step up. Overtures have been expanding for a while: Beethoven's 'Egmont' and 'Coriolan' are chunky dishes on their own, then Mendelssohn swaggers in with his 'Hebrides' overture and the high-seas drama of 'Fingal's Cave', and then Berlioz with the picture-painting epic of 'Le Corsaire' overture, and the scene is definitely set. It's a nice irony as the overture became the symphony and now the symphony is turning back into a dramatic and glamorous overture.

Do you remember, from quite a while back, we talked about the shape or form of a piece of music? One of the most common forms for overtures is the sonata: two main characters, they do a bunch of stuff in the development, and at the end for the recapitulation we meet up with them again and they're all grown up. Well, that form is about to be chucked in the bin as a musician, sorry, a super-musician, called Franz Liszt bursts onto the scene. He starts quietly enough, with overtures in the regular shape, but then that shape becomes increasingly, shall we say, unpredictable. Within a decade, Liszt pushes the concept of a single movement orchestral piece beyond an overture and composes twelve of what are now called symphonic or tone poems. And with this music Liszt brings the outside world back into the concert hall, giving the music a story and character and making more conservative composers like Brahms look, frankly, a bit dull.

Liszt's 'The Battle of the Huns' is a good example. He gives this instruction in the score: 'Conductors: the entire colour should be kept very dark, and all instruments must sound like ghosts.' You don't get that with Brahms.

Any talk about tone poems must also include Richard Strauss and his epics: 'Don Juan', with its almost unplayable beginning; 'A Hero's Life', which makes the horn even more heroic than it was already; and 'Till Eulenspiegel's Merry Pranks', which brings the orchestra to the rumpus room. Ooh, and 'Death and Transfiguration' — talk about a good title for this chapter. Now we have no constraints about what to put where, which chord to end on or how many times we need to play a certain theme.

Claude Debussy continues to break every rule with his 'Prelude to the Afternoon of a Faun', also a tone poem, and George Gershwin and his 'An American in Paris'. And don't forget Paul Dukas and 'The Sorcerer's Apprentice'. Who knew? Music is now coming together with cartoons.

The one thing about these symphonic poems, though, is that they don't last long. Well, they literally last about ten or fifteen minutes, but the fashion for writing them fades by the late 1920s.

So they are a bright, fast-burning light that illuminates our way into the twentieth century.

Sir Edward Elgar, 'In the South'

This is classed as an overture *and* a tone poem, and it has a glorious viola solo. You'll be glad when you hear that tune.

Edward Elgar's music stands out in this liminal sound of the nineteenth and twentieth centuries: in one moment he is inside a hedge lining a lane in the middle of a bucolic pastoral scene (his Serenade for Strings), in another he is debating the deepest theosophical ideas with his 'The Dream of Gerontius', and in another he is weeping for generations (his Cello Concerto). Elgar has a suppleness of thought and creativity that is matched by very few. All of this and he is English to boot, at a time when English music is considered a little sluggish and dull.

Perhaps one of the reasons Elgar manages to shake off that English tempering is travel — to Germany, North and South America (he travels up the Amazon) and frequently to Italy, where he composes this work. 'In the South' may not be quite south enough, though, as Elgar goes to Alassio on the Ligurian coast of Italy in December when it is freezing, windy and rainy, and he complains bitterly about the bitterness. Doh.

This piece is like trying to move a mattress on your own: unwieldy, seemingly impossible, and yet, when you have done it, wildly satisfying. Elgar uses the full symphony orchestra in a glare of Italian light, with none of that English politeness and a lot of big English roast taste. This is music for a Dickens version of Italy, except for that sublime viola solo towards the end.

You might feel, at around the eighteen-minute mark, that perhaps it's time to stop this feasting as we really cannot eat anymore. Now music is starting to feel too full, overinflated, congested even. Something is going to have to shift.

38

WTF

WTF.

Hang on, that's a bit rude, isn't it? This is a classical music book!

Ah yes, sorry, but WTF doesn't mean quite what you think it does here. We are now at the very beginning of the twentieth century and the message of WTF is 'welcome, tonal freedom'! Sounds huge, right? But this seismic change in music isn't surprising considering the current frenetic pace of change in society: Marconi receives the first transatlantic radio signal, the Wright brothers go for a heavier-than-air very short flight, the Trans-Siberian Railway and Panama Canal begin construction, and two things that will change the course of history are brought into the world: $E = mc^2$ and ... wait for it, wait for it ... teddy bears! (Hello, Mr Scruffy.)

To match this evolutionary whirl (and that's just the teddy bears), there's more rapid change with harmony and melody in European music. So much change that it will be impossible to stuff the strict rules of tonal harmony back in their well-made suitcase.

Just to remind you, tonality is the concept of home and away chords, and the journey between. We need balance to have that beautiful feeling of tension and release (think TV soap operas, only better) but now, after the Late Romantics (those lazy love interests) and the about-to-burst-onto-the-scene game-changer jazz, tonality can no longer be relied upon. In fact, tonality is about as fashionable these days as a tonsure. People want excitement, aural travel, a new perspective! Forget fustiness and even the vaguest hint of predictability. That's so last century.

The first few years of the twentieth century herald the huge variety of music to come. In 1900 alone, one of the greatest playlists, sorry, operas ever, Giacomo Puccini's *Tosca*, is premiered, as well as a deeply religious masterpiece, 'The Dream of Gerontius' by Sir Edward Elgar. And in 1905, the widening gap between styles is even more evident: in this year you can hear Arnold Schoenberg's 'Pelleas and Melisande', where tonality is seriously having a fag out the back of the building, Gustav Mahler's gaunt *Kindertotenlieder* and Franz Lehár's operetta *The Merry Widow*. A good guide to whether these pieces use tonality is if you can whistle them afterwards. Also, would you want to whistle them afterwards? Of these pieces, only *The Merry Widow* stands a chance.

But perhaps the composer who shines the most in these early years of the 1900s is Igor Stravinsky. Although there is one night in Paris, in 1913, when he is perhaps less shining and more glistening from the tomatoes that are being chucked at him.

Let's backtrack a little …

As the 1900s arrive, so does eighteen-year-old Igor at law school in St Petersburg. Igor closes his law books quite quickly, hangs out with the son of Russia's most famous composer, Rimsky-Korsakov, and starts to study music with him. The dad that is. Not quite sure what he does with the son. In 1910, the ballet impresario Sergei Diaghilev hears some of Stravinsky's music and invites him to compose for the Ballets Russes Paris season. And so it is that on 29 May 1913, Stravinsky's ballet *The Rite of Spring*, subtitled 'Pictures of Pagan Russia in Two Parts', is premiered.

Even though musical systems have been transforming for a while, nothing can prepare the ear or even the spirit for *The Rite of Spring*. Has the shock of it ever been surpassed? A riot follows the first performance. The music seems to come from the earth itself — the wild and visceral harmonies, the mutated folk music, the textures and the brutal rhythms that disturb everything within and without. Modernism has come to music, with the small irony that to access the future, Stravinsky has looked back to the ancients.

You hear that sound? That's tonality being waved out the door. Also tomatoes being chucked by the audience.

Lili Boulanger, 'Of a Sad Evening'

The Boulanger sisters, Nadia and Lili, have a momentous effect on music in the twentieth century. Nadia, the older sister, will teach some of the great composers of this time, and yes, that includes Quincy Jones. She is described as 'the greatest teacher since Socrates' and lives until she is ninety-two. Lili will hardly live to enjoy adulthood, dying from intestinal tuberculosis at the age of twenty-four.

Despite her youth, Lili has already won the biggest scholarship prize of them all, the Grand Prix de Rome (she is the first female winner), with a cantata called 'Faust et Hélène'. Lili studies at the Paris Conservatoire under Gabriel Fauré, who is a big fan of hers. You can only imagine his grief at her early death.

This piece is composed in 1918, just months before she dies; it's part of a diptych with another orchestral poem, 'Of a Spring Morning'. Due to Lili's illness, this is the last piece she will be able to write without her sister's help; the manuscript is faint and difficult to read. After Lili's death, Nadia files the manuscript away and it isn't seen for sixty years.

The sound harks back to parallel organum and forward to a breakdown of the harmonic rules so carefully built by (mostly) men over the last two hundred years. Lili, such a profound and complex musician, is able to access all the sounds and textures she wants, and with her wise processing of the machinery of music, we are left with this consummate work. Stravinsky yells and screams and cajoles, but Lili doesn't need to do any of that. Her music is more a declaration than an argument. There is an imperious, strange logic to her work. The music folds in on itself after the exuberance and over-indulgence of Stravinsky and Elgar. With this sad evening, Lili is drawing the curtains on the world and on her own life.

39

There is nothing like
a Dame (Ethyl Smyth)

Holloway Prison, London, 1911
Sound of clanking doors and locks, keys, distant sound of women
singing

ELB: Good morning! I'm here to visit Ethyl Smyth — she
was imprisoned a few days ago?
Guard: Smyth? Oh gosh. Yes. Smyth. Blimey, I wish they
'adn't brought 'er 'ere. That woman is causing a serious
disturbance, making a racket with all that singing. I'll
see if she wants a visitor. That bloke Thomas Beecham
was round 'ere yesterday — 'e only made it worse. Bloody
musicians. Always makin' some sort o' noise, they are.
ELB: Well, thank you. I'll just wait here?
Guard: That's it. And you're dressed funny, where you
from then?

ELB: Oh, I'm from the future. Maybe tell Miss Smyth that.
Then she might want to talk with me.
Guard: Righto. Blimey, I see some bloody odd things 'ere,
I do ...

One hour later ...

Ethyl Smyth (to guard): I tell you, my good woman, there
is a rat in my cell. How can I compose when all I can hear
is scratching and gnawing? Good morning — who are you
and for which journal do you write?
ELB (hastily standing and bowing): Good morning, Dame
Ethyl. I'm Ed Le Brocq from the Australian Broadcasting
Corporation — I'm from the future and I wondered if I
could ask you a few questions?
ES: Dame? Ha, I shall never be damed. Damned, more
likely. What is a broadcast corporation? Oh never mind,
you're clearly not of sound mind from your haircut, but
some people say I'm not either, so we may as well have a
little talk. Not too long, mind, I need to get back to my cell
and see Emmeline.
ELB: Ah, Emmeline Pankhurst! Wow. Well, thank you,
and actually, you will be made a dame in 1922. I wanted
to ask you about your childhood ... Was your dad a very
model of a modern major-general?
ES: Hmm, I appreciate your quoting of Gilbert and
Sullivan — Sullivan has been a great help to me —
but no, Papa was not at all modern. We had the most

vicious arguments when I was a gal, but in the end he allowed me to study music in Leipzig and I met the most extraordinary people ...

ELB: Yes! You met Tchaikovsky and Clara Schumann?

ES: I most certainly did. Grieg as well, and Dvořák. A lovely man. Smelled of horses. Of course, they all had the good fortune of meeting me, I'd rather think. Wouldn't you?

ELB: Absolutely. Dame Ethyl, you have said that if you compose like a man, you are criticised for being manly, but if you compose like a woman, you are criticised for being too womanly. Is there a catch-22 of composing?

ES: I don't know what a catch-22 is but there is certainly a conundrum. I decided a long time ago to compose how I wanted to, which I suppose is rather as men do. I am simply myself.

ELB: There are some remarkable myths about you still, over a hundred years from now ... Is it true you tied yourself to a tree once? If so, why?

ES: Ah yes, one must have excellent posture. Otherwise, one will not be taken seriously.

ELB: And is it true you taught Emmeline Pankhurst to throw stones through windows?

ES: Yes, that is also true. And my word, Emmeline has a dreadful throw. We planned to go and break some windows in Westminster for the suffragettes and crowd out the prisons when we would all be arrested. I think there were to be one hundred and fifty of us ... Anyway, I took

Emmeline to Hook Heath one night to practise, collected a pile of stones and told Emmeline to aim at a large fir tree. She almost hit my poor dog on her first try. It seems she was aiming at fur, not fir. She hit the tree once in about fifty attempts. This woman did not play ball games in her youth. When we finally went window-breaking, Emmeline missed her target. I, of course, did not. Yet here we both are. Emmeline is next door. The matron lets us see each other most days. She even locks us in Emmeline's cell together and 'forgets' to come and fetch me.

ELB: Oh, that's very kind of her. You know, at the end of your life you're going to be worried, not about dying but about your music. That it will die with you. Well, Dame Ethyl, it doesn't. In fact, there are more and more performances every year, and one of your works, *The Prison*, wins a Grammy!

ES: I have no idea what a Grammy is but I am so very happy to hear that about my music. Thank you. Now, I must get back to my work. By the way, do you happen to have a spare toothbrush? I dropped mine the other day conducting my march for women.

Dame Ethyl Smyth, 'The March of the Women'

'I arrived in the main courtyard to find the noble company of martyrs marching round it and singing lustily their war-chant while the composer, beaming approbation from an overlooking upper window, beat time in almost Bacchic frenzy with a toothbrush.'

The words of Sir Thomas Beecham after visiting Ethyl Smyth in Holloway Prison. Ethyl Smyth's 'The March of the Women' is officially presented to the suffragettes of the Women's Social and Political Union on 23 March 1911 at the Royal Albert Hall in London. Dame Ethyl has decided to dedicate two years of her life to the suffragette movement and work with her lover, Emmeline Pankhurst, to win universal suffrage. The motto of the union is 'Deeds Not Words', and Smyth contributes with her best deeds by teaching Emmeline to chuck bricks through windows and composing this anthem.

During these suffragette years, Smyth doesn't keep her usual meticulous diary, but she does eventually write about the event where the anthem is presented: how she composes the music first and Cicely Hamilton, writer and actor, creates the words afterwards, how one of the choir members complains about an E flat and the interval to get there (a minor third – the first two notes of 'Greensleeves'), how a cornet and an organ are there to bash out the tune, how Ethyl and Emmeline walk up the central aisle of the Royal Albert Hall and how Ethyl is presented with a golden baton.

Everything about this march is well made: the clear, stout harmony, the sensible rhythm, the no-nonsense words with the inimitable first line: 'Shout, shout, up with your song'. This is an anthem and a battle cry.

Women are given the vote in the United Kingdom in 1918, but it is limited to women over thirty, and with strict property rules. Equal suffrage is not won until 1928.

40

Impressions and expressions

Winter, 1914. A man has just walked out of an army recruiting office after being accepted as a private in the Royal Army Medical Corps, despite being forty-two years old. Within weeks Ralph Vaughan Williams will be in France driving ambulances, walking through gore and mud, trying to save the dying.

How does art of any sort ever convey the slaughter and catastrophe of the First World War? Visual art may, with artists like Arthur Streeton and John Singer Sargent, but it's the photographs that sear and stick. Frank Hurley's *Hellfire Corner*, taken in 1917, is an image of the futility and impossibility of war.

And so it is with music, which looks at this central calamity from varying perspectives. In 1914 we hear the cheerful 'Colonel Bogey March', Scott Joplin's ironic 'Magnetic Rag', Zoltan Kodaly's caustic Duo for Violin and Cello, Maurice Ravel's tragic Piano Trio and Frederick Delius's diaphanous Violin Sonata.

Delius is writing music in a style now known as impressionism, despite the main composer in this style,

Claude Debussy, saying that anyone who calls it that is basically an idiot. Tough words, but you can hear why the term is used.

If you think back to tonality and its use of particular notes in a chord, you remember how they align with the primary colours; in impressionism, those notes are changing from the primary to secondary and even tertiary colours. Debussy and other composers like Lili Boulanger and Paul Dukas are turning away from European, especially Germanic, influences and towards the east with their use of the pentatonic scale. This is prompted by the 1889 Paris Exhibition, where Debussy hears Javanese gamelan music for the first time. 'Stairway to Heaven', 'Auld Lang Syne' and 'Amazing Grace' are just some of the Western songs that use this scale, and you can hear how the music is looser, more pliant. So from a clearly painted, often taut musical landscape of the 1800s, now the sound is slacker, more lenient somehow.

Debussy has this to say about music: 'I am more and more convinced that music, by its very nature, is something that cannot be cast into a traditional and fixed form. It is made up of colours and rhythms.'

Tonality, over thousands of years, has been built in a case that was incubated by the Ancient Greeks, developed by the English, codified by the French, styled by the Italians and perfected by the Germans. Now, during the war to end all wars, music is turning to the past, to the parallel harmonies of the mediaeval age, to the modes of the Ancient Greeks and to the even older sounds of Asia.

Impressionistic music describes the vibe, the atmosphere of an event or place, but it's not long before music catches up with explorations into psychology and we turn inward to examine ourselves — the dissonance and distortion of expressionism and atonalism are just around the corner.

Claude Debussy, 'The Submerged Cathedral', Préludes, Book I

How can sounds produced by a felt hammer on steel strings induce in us a feeling of sinking, dropping deeper and deeper into the depths of the ocean? Because this is where Claude Debussy's prelude 'La cathédrale engloutie (The Submerged Cathedral)' takes us.

Debussy composes his first book of preludes in 1909, each a tiny, intense scene: 'La fille aux cheveux de lin (The Girl with the Flaxen Hair)' is a sound portrait of youthful beauty; 'Des pas sur la neige (Footsteps in the Snow)' a trudge through deep, endless winter; 'Le vent dans la plaine (The Wind in the Plain)' a bitter race to warmth. And this psychological metaphor, the weight, the sheer mass of the cathedral, becoming a burden around our necks as it lifts us and ultimately drags us down.

This prelude is a musical sketch of the mythical island of Ys and its cathedral, which is said to rise out of the sea off the coast of Brittany when the weather is fine. The wide chords at the beginning of the piece reach back to mediaeval harmony with their parallel notes, creating both a horizon and a structure, and that openness sings on with a depiction of bells peeling and monks chanting. Debussy includes the instruction to 'emerge from the fog, little by little'. You can hear the influence of the

Russian Five on Debussy; there's a pagan beat to this music, even if a cathedral is at its heart. The whole piece is a giant arc, as the cathedral with its organ sounding emerges and slowly sinks below the water again.

Throughout this book there are composers who have officially studied their craft and composers who are self-taught. Debussy is a composer who has studied all the details of Western classical music and, through learning what he *should* be doing, can properly decide what he really *wants* to do. There is perhaps a clearer line from Debussy to cubism rather than impressionism. Debussy is not turning his back on tonality, as Arnold Schoenberg is about to do. Debussy is taking us further along the path of tonality.

But in the end, what does all matter? As Debussy says, 'There is no theory. You have only to listen. Pleasure is the law.'

41

Every note is equal

You know that feeling, when walking through a hall of mirrors at a fairground, and your reflection from mirror to mirror gradually moves further away from reality and comprehension? Is that, is this, really you?

This is one way of illustrating the movement of tonality in the early 1900s.

Another way is through colour.

Those bright, clear primary colours of established harmony are gradually being blurred and made more complex. As Sigmund Freud and his psychoanalytic examinations into the ego and the id are becoming more widely known, so we understand more of the ambiguity of ourselves, and music is becoming more ambiguous. The sense of where and who we are is harder to find. The same change in form and line is expressed in art — think Pablo Picasso and his *Weeping Woman*, her shape and grief reduced to geometry, James Joyce and his novel *Ulysses* — but here instead of reduction we have the explosion of a moment, a feeling.

Who could not be influenced by these new paths and laneways of thinking? When Austrian-American composer Arnold Schoenberg starts to walk off the path of tonality into the woodlands of atonality, a seismic break is made in the history of music, perhaps the most important since those skittish monks back in the 1000s with their parallel organum.

Because now, there is no hierarchy in music.

Instead of the hierarchy of the home note and its chord based on the primary colours, we can now have any note, at any time, with any other note. It's essentially chaos theory in music. But if you're going to have that, well, you might as well just have chaos, so Schoenberg decides that there does indeed need to be some sort of order, and that's how his so-called twelve-tone technique comes to life. It's also called serialism, or the Second Viennese School. Mozart and Haydn are the first, and they would like you to remember that.

You also remember since way back with the Harappans and the Ancient Greeks we have been using a system of notes where the octave is divided into seven. It's called the diatonic scale and is a mix of whole tones ('Happy Birthday') and semitones (*Jaws*). In many parts of Asia five notes are used in an octave, and that's called the pentatonic scale (there are no semitones, so you can relax about the sharks). Over time other notes have been added, but generally a whistle-able tune has a diatonic or pentatonic base.

But here comes Arnie. He decides that he will use all the half steps, or semitones, in an octave, that makes twelve notes, and with them he will create a foundation for a piece of music; he calls this foundation a tone row. He creates the rule that the tone row *must* use all twelve notes, and then he manipulates the tone row in various ways.

To illustrate this musical system, here's possibly the most famous sentence in Western literature, which conveniently has twelve words (thanks, Mr Orwell). For our tone row we have: *Every animal is equal, but some animals are more equal than others.*

Backwards, it becomes: *Others than equal more are animals some but equal is animal every.*

Now we'll skip a word, and then go back a word, so now it becomes: *Every is animal equal but animals some are more than equal others.*

Then we make that backwards, and it now becomes: *Others equal than more are some animals but equal animal is every.*

Until in the end the manipulations, as they go on and on, can either take you very far away or start to bring you back to the beginning. It's a highly regimented way of creating music and, to be honest, it hasn't exactly caught on in the dance halls. However, this new way of thinking about music, of letting go of the hierarchy, allows composers completely free reign.

After Schoenberg, there need never be any rules ever again.

Arnold Schoenberg, *Two Pieces*, Op. 33

By the time Arnold Schoenberg composes these two piano pieces in 1931, he has already composed music with tonality, gradually pushed that tonality into atonality, and briefly come back to tonality again. No surprise he is famous; when he is called up to fight in the First World War (just like Ralph Vaughan Williams, he's forty-two), an army officer asks him if he is the notorious Schoenberg. 'Beg to report, sir, yes. Nobody wanted to be, someone had to be, so I let it be me.'

Arnold is then put in charge of a military band. You've got to wonder what music they play.

Music so often has diverging sounds in the same era, and it's strange to think that Edward Elgar's Cello Concerto is written a few years after these pieces. There could hardly be more disparate approaches to music and yet, in their own way, both these works are highly romantic. It's just that the Schoenberg pieces go to extremes of romanticism with wild dynamics, alarming phrase lengths and disparate moods, all distilled into two tiny universes. Despite its extremity, Schoenberg directs that the music be played 'moderately' and 'moderately slowly'. Hardly ground-breaking, until the music begins.

It seems odd to say but there really is a clear conversation with this music. This is language. Sure, it is a hard-to-understand, even a do-you-want-to-understand-it language, but this music is communicating with us. It quarries into our minds, into our cells, a doubt here, an unknown elation there, seducing us in strange ways. Of course, we don't find this music easy. Schoenberg is going against the natural laws of the universe and the structure of the harmonic series, the series that Jean-Philippe Rameau so devotedly established. But perhaps the point of Schoenberg's music is that, just as people will always question the status quo, if we do not have Schoenberg, where would our music be going? Do we want to always be stuck in a predictable series of chords, an endless elevator music of blah blah blah?

For a man who stands out so defiantly, Schoenberg has some surprising stories. He accepts his rent being paid by Mahler, rejects a stipend from Brahms, leaves Berlin in 1933 and ends up living in Los Angeles in a Spanish Revival villa opposite Shirley Temple, has Harpo Marx round for tea and plays tennis with George Gershwin. He also teaches film music at UCLA, which we will investigate a little more in a few chapters' time.

And finally, all his life Schoenberg is afraid of the number thirteen — it's called triskaidekaphobia. He dies in Los Angeles on Friday, 13 July 1951 at the age of seventy-six.

$7 + 6 = 13$

42

The soundtrack of protest

One theme that sings through this book is how crucial, how central, music is to humanity. From the Mesopotamians and their love songs in 4000 BCE, to Beethoven and his rage against the machine and now Schoenberg and his mates with their experiments into the limits of music, this line of song and sound vibrates through nearly all our lives. And political leaders know this power and try to suppress it.

As the 1920s party on, the relief of the postwar period descends into financial calamity, with hyperinflation in Germany meaning you need a wheelbarrow of money to buy a loaf of bread. In the United States, the Harlem Renaissance brings to international prominence musicians like Fats Waller, Jelly Roll Morton, Duke Ellington, Florence Price, William Grant Still and Louis Armstrong. *The Jazz Singer* is the first movie to use a synchronised recorded music score as sound recording is becoming fully electric.

The world markets finally crash in 1929, throwing the

Western world into the Great Depression. Stalin takes power in the Soviet Union, quantum chemistry is developed and Schrödinger and his cat are both alive and dead.

It's a good time to be alive. Or dead.

Kurt Weill, the composer, and the librettist Berthold Brecht come to typify the artistic criticism and opposition to the German economy and government. Their cynical *Threepenny Opera*, a rebuke of the capitalist system, premieres in 1928, but it's not long before Nazi groups target the pair and theatres decline to stage the work. As the Nazis take over in Germany and Italy, more and more artists have their work labelled as degenerate. The Nazis even create degenerate art and degenerate music shows that tour around Germany, with images of the artists and composers and listening booths where you can hear their music. The artists are banned from being performed or shown (except by the Nazis), and these people, if they are fortunate, begin to leave Europe for safer places, especially the US. As radio becomes a central part of the Nazi propaganda machine, music is vetted and only 'real German' music is broadcast. Definitely no Schoenberg.

In the Soviet Union, Dmitri Shostakovich struggles with the steel-capped-boot control of the Communist Party, yet he walks a fine line of suitability and rebellion with his operas and symphonies. Everything is going well until his opera *Lady Macbeth of Mtsensk* is criticised by the Soviet government in the newspaper *Pravda*. Shostakovich spends the next three years terrified, sleeping in his clothes, worrying, believing he is about to be sent to Siberia. Only in 1937 with his Fifth Symphony, subtitled 'An Artist's Response to Just Criticism', does he find a tiny fleck of artistic safety. The savagery and cynicism of this life soak into every note of Shostakovich. We listen to his music and we feel the chill of the stairwell where he sleeps, the fear of the street where people ignore him, the passion of an artist who needs to speak.

Kurt Weill, Paul Hindemith, Béla Bartók, Igor Stravinsky and Arnold Schoenberg are just some of the banned musicians who manage to leave Europe. So many do not, so many cannot. Composers and musicians, either because of their ethnicity, their sexuality or their work, are taken to concentration camps and murdered. Here are a mere few: Dora Gerson is an actor and singer who is gassed at Auschwitz; Arnold Siméon van Wesel is a jazz singer who dies in Bergen-Belsen; Pavel Haas, a composer, is gassed in Auschwitz; Erwin Schulhoff, a composer and jazz pianist, dies in Wülzburg concentration camp; Alma Rosé, violinist, impresario, niece of Gustav Mahler, leader of

THE SOUNDTRACK OF PROTEST

the Women's Orchestra of Auschwitz, dies of food poisoning in Auschwitz-Birkenau. The film *Playing for Time* is made about this band beyond bravery. This is an unimaginable loss that we *must* imagine, because we must remember.

The rise of Nazism in Europe brings cut and spite to music, but there is another direction as well, a turn to the past, with Stravinsky, Ottorino Respighi, Maurice Ravel and Sergei Prokofiev looking to classical music and reimagining it with their neoclassical works, like Respighi's *Ancient Airs and Dances* and Stravinsky's ballet *Pulcinella*. There are so few safe places in Europe now but one is England, to where many refugees flee. England has once been called, by a German, 'the land without music', but now all these refugee musicians hasten the changes that within decades will turn England into the heart of music-making in Europe.

And in the United States, as the Empire State and Chrysler buildings go up, and up, then up quite a bit more, musicians come to this land of hope, singing their songs. And those songs are about to become some of the most famous ever written when music becomes the musical.

Alban Berg, Violin Concerto

Four strings. Four sounds. The DNA of music, of the violin, and from there everything springs forth. This is the opening of Alban Berg's Violin Concerto, composed in 1935 and written in memory of Manon Gropius, daughter of Alma Mahler and Walter Gropius: 'To the memory of an angel.' Manon is nineteen when she dies from polio.

Alban Berg is one of the composers whose music is banned by the Nazis, who state that it is diseased and against the state. Just how music can be against the state is hard to figure, but Berg is probably glad to be against this particular state. Berg is a student of Arnold Schoenberg and takes on his twelve-tone technique, although the student uses it in other intensely sweet ways.

So here we are with our tone row at the beginning of the Violin Concerto. You remember that we have twelve semitones, and we must use each one once, otherwise Schoenberg will get cross. This could end up sounding cacophonous (the tone row *and* Schoenberg), but Berg organises these notes into little parcels of tonal meaning, so that we have three chords that Jean-Philippe Rameau would be proud of, and the final four notes are the first four of a Bach chorale, 'Es ist genug' (It is Enough). With this music, Berg makes a breakthrough in tonality/atonality, a breakthrough that synthesises the past and the future and brings sublime beauty into a hideous world.

43

Now that's a tune!

And it's showtime! Here we are in 1927 at the Ziegfeld Theatre in New York City for the premiere of *Show Boat*. With music by Jerome Kern, lyrics by Oscar Hammerstein and 'Ol' Man River' sung by a nobody who will very quickly become a somebody, Paul Robeson, *Show Boat* is the opener for a whole new era of music: the exploration of serious contemporary issues through song, dialogue and dance, otherwise known as the musical.

What makes a musical? How is it different from an opera or operetta? Well, it really comes down to perspective. We need songs, quite a lot of them, we need dialogue throughout to move the story forward, and speaking of moving, we need dancing. Sometimes these three are happening at the same time, and if you're Hugh Jackman, you pull it and your shirt off with absolutely no trouble.

So even though *Show Boat* is the first to perfectly balance all those elements, the Ancient Greeks kind of got there first with dance and music in their ancient plays about ancient stuff. In mediaeval times, wagons full of musicians would travel around performing biblical plays with song, and moving through the centuries we see and hear plays with music from the 1500s in England, to Molière and Lully in France in the 1700s, and comic opera in Italy throughout the 1800s. Jacques Offenbach and Johann Strauss II create light opera, or operetta, where the 'humability' of the tunes and the comic aspect of the stories mould a serious feeling of fluffiness. W.S. Gilbert and Arthur Sullivan in Britain do the same with masterpieces like *HMS Pinafore* and *The Pirates of Penzance* (yes, it is easy to confuse pilots and pirates).

The first musical theatre in New York is called The Black Crook. With street lighting installed in the late 1800s, the city at night changes from a dangerous place to a place of magic, and now theatre has moved away from saucy burlesque with skimpy clothing to clean, family entertainment. The upheavals of the First World War in Europe are bringing more and more immigrants to the US, and with them they bring a taste and desire for quality entertainment. The Roaring Twenties, the need for release and escape, foment vaudeville and musical revues and make stars of people like Fred Astaire and Cole Porter. But it's with *Show Boat* that we finally have a thrilling, important story to be told, a story of segregation, racism and prejudice. And there are some stunning songs to tell that story, like 'Ol' Man River'.

Now, with the use of a 'book', or the script and stage directions, a musical has clear structure and music motifs, just like with Wagner or Verdi. And as the out-of-control twenties

NOW THAT'S A TUNE!

move to the Great Depression thirties, musicals take on a political sheen with George Gershwin's *Porgy and Bess* and the political satire *Of Thee I Sing*, and Kurt Weill's *Knickerbocker Holiday*.

The golden era of musicals in the United States coincides with a lift in the economy and the nation's entry into the Second World War. The contrasts are shocking: European cities are being obliterated, millions are being murdered in concentration camps and Schoenberg is experimenting with his twelve-tone technique, yet Rogers and Hammerstein's *Oklahoma!* opens with the song 'Oh, What a Beautiful Mornin'' as one character churns butter. Perhaps it's no surprise that in this time of horror beyond thought, a story of love in the safety of a corn field will have a run of over two thousand performances and win a Pulitzer Prize.

Rodgers and Hammerstein will go on to write *Carousel* and *South Pacific* and will inspire composers all the way through to Andrew Lloyd Webber with *Jesus Christ Superstar* and Lin-Manuel Miranda with *Hamilton*.

With every show, musical theatre sings to us that at the heart of everything is simply a good story and a good tune.

Richard Rodgers and Oscar Hammerstein II, *Oklahoma!*

Millions are dying in Europe, Asia and parts of Africa in ways unimaginable just a few years before. Yet in the United States, a man called Curly is riding a horse across a theatre stage through fake corn stalks, singing about the beauty of the day and how easy life is. There isn't a tone row in sight, only corn rows. It's one of the great moments in music history not because of what we hear but because of what we don't hear.

Why is this music so successful? In many ways, it shouldn't have been; one of the producers in the early test runs walks out, quipping, 'No girls, no gags, no chance.' Yet in 1944 *Oklahoma!* wins a special Pulitzer Prize and goes on to a run of more than two thousand performances, a hit movie and endless reruns. The show is stuffed full of great tunes — 'The Surrey with a Fringe on Top', 'People Will Say We're in Love', 'All Er Nuthin'' — and each one releases a little puff of endorphins. We want to sing along, we want to dance, we are happy with the happiness of others. We can turn from the internal investigation of atonal music to a simple enjoyment of the external, with a safe and secure home note, homemade butter in the pantry and corn on the cob for dinner.

For decades leading to here, Claude Debussy, Arnold Schoenberg, Lili Boulanger and others have all been standing in the tonality tent, pushing the walls out until they fray and split. Richard Rodgers stands in the tonality tent and doesn't push at all. In fact, he is so tent-content that he sits down in a comfy chair and stretches out his legs. Richard Rodgers, from his cushioned position in the safe United States, understands that music can either scrutinise humanity's collapse or celebrate humanity's joy. And surely we should do the latter while we still can.

44

What's *Psycho* without the soundtrack?

Two notes. Just two tiny notes and with them one of the great villains of film comes flooding into our mind, our psyche. Watch out for the mechanical shark! Fortunately, it's not only fear that film music brings — it can also usher in love, nostalgia, hope and resolve. And the developments in film music very much match the developments in music throughout the twentieth century.

In the late nineteenth century, film technology doesn't yet allow for synchronised sound, so film nights will literally be, well, quiet. One could even say silent, so musicians are paid to fill in the silences with music suggested by the films' producers. Some composers such as Camille Saint-Saëns and Edmund Meisel compose special music to be played alongside the silent films, music that is played by musicians such as young Dimitri Shostakovich in the Soviet Union. It isn't until the 1930s and the advent of talkies that the first film score, for *King Kong*, is composed by Max Steiner, someone who has just been let go by his studio and will go on to be called the father of film music.

It's true that musicians can be, shall we say, particular, but they are really no more particular than costume designers or makeup artists, so it's pretty unfair that film producers in the 1930s blame production delays on their films' music and try to do without it. It isn't until people see that music is clearly beneficial to a film's success that it becomes de rigeur to have a film score. And with Max Steiner's influence, the music has as much rigour and cohesiveness as any piece of classical music, using leitmotifs or themes for separate characters and bringing a new psychological depth to the drama on screen. Christoph Willibald Gluck is beaming from all those centuries ago.

As European composers escape revolution and persecution and slowly arrive in Hollywood, composers like Igor Stravinsky, Erich Wolfgang Korngold and Arnold Schoenberg are invited to write for the silver screen. In fact, Schoenberg — yes, that Schoenberg of the twelve-tone method — becomes a professor of composition at UCLA, a renowned film school. So when you hear the majesty and harmonic daring of Bernard Herrmann, Alfred Hitchcock's go-to man for psychological drama, these worlds all begin to make sense and come together. What is the shower scene in *Psycho* without the music? Okay, it's still scary, but now all you need to hear is that screeching violin and you're immediately quaking in your shower cap. Images on their own do not elicit music in our imagination, but music on its own does elicit mental imagery.

Film music uses the classical music soundscape, expands into jazz and folk music, and with Ennio Morricone and his Spaghetti Western soundscapes uses one of the most commonplace of instruments, the harmonica — now film music is available to anyone with room in their back pocket. From the 1960s, theme songs are crucial to a film's success through regular radio play, songs like 'Moon River' from *Breakfast at Tiffany's* and 'Goldfinger' from, er, *Goldfinger.*

As musicians start to use synthesisers and computers, they play their way into film. What would that scene of blokes jogging down a rainy beach in *Chariots of Fire* be without Vangelis and his da da da da da da da da da da da da da on the synthesiser? (Although one of the most famous films, Hitchcock's *The Birds*, has only bird shrieks as its soundtrack, a noise that really concentrates the mind.) And there surely can never be a more compelling sound to make us sit and watch and stay as that opening chord to *Star Wars*; its resonance goes beyond the world, out of the galaxy and into the universe, opening our minds to adventure. Because the music in films does what the action can never really do and *that* is take us to another dimension.

Bernard Herrmann, *Vertigo*

We have learned about diatonic scales and the intensity of the semitone interval (the shark is full now, you can relax for a bit), and you now know about how harmony can mercilessly turn the lights off and beatifically turn them on again. Harmony, the shading under a melody, is at the heart of Western music, and Bernard Herrmann is one of its crusaders.

When you think of the scores for films like *Psycho*, *North by Northwest*, *Cape Fear*, *The Man Who Knew Too Much* and *Taxi Driver*, the name Percy Grainger does not necessarily come to mind. The man who makes arrangements of the folk tune 'Country Gardens' doesn't exactly sit side by side the man who drills us with fear in a single violin chord. But when you think beyond Grainger's folk music and consider his experimental music, including aleatoric music (of chance) and his works with a rapidly changing pulse, things begin to make sense. And that's not even considering Percy's predilection for personal punishment. Here's possibly a surprise: Percy Grainger is one of Bernard Herrmann's teachers at New York University.

It's 1958, the cinema lights have gone down, the news reel has finished and the film begins. The opening of *Vertigo*. A series of kaleidoscopic images, sometimes turning anti-clockwise, sometimes flattening their perspective, sometimes becoming a human eye, sometimes drawing us into a vortex. And all the time, Herrmann's series of chords leaches into our darkest places and chills our very spinal fluid. How can this happen?

Because there is no home note.

A home note can be an aural resting place; it is our ground, it is our balance point, and with those opening shots and chords we are left swirling in the air with constant tension. Tension in music is often created with the use of a technique called suspension. Imagine you are on a ladder and it slips. You grab hold of the guttering you were fixing and manage to get two hands up, but your legs are dangling in mid-air ten metres above the ground. How do you feel? Probably a little unhappy. You try to swing your legs up onto the roof, but you will only relax when the whole of you is on the roof, not just your arms. Suspension in music is the same, as some notes move to the next place but some are left perilously behind. It's a technique that Richard Wagner uses in the opera *Tristan and Isolde* — the opening chord never truly resolves for four and half hours. In this, and in *Vertigo*, we have a sense of coming in sideways, or coming in halfway through ... what have we missed? What should we do? Am I safe? In this music, the suspension and tension are only briefly resolved, and even then it is with a chord that makes you want to wash your hands. This is sullied music, and that makes it even more thrilling.

Herrmann takes all the harmonic history of Western music and puts it in this score. Carlo Gesualdo and his murderous colours, the pentatonic shading of Claude Debussy, the tiny motifs of Jean Sibelius, the flaying of the Second Viennese School, the orchestration of the Romantics and the briefest bathing of tonality. Even a suggestion of the minimalism to come.

The plot of the movie is summed up concisely by the director, Sir Alfred Hitchcock, himself: 'To put it plainly, the man wants to go to bed with a woman who is dead.' This film is a love story, but it must be one of the queerest ever told, and without Herrmann's score we would not experience that same density of anxiety. This music saturates our mind with dread until it crystalises.

Hitchcock knows the power of the score. In one of the film's love scenes he notes in the script: 'Keep the sound down here, because I believe Mr Herrmann will have something to say.'

He does. Yet Bernard Herrmann also knows the power of silence.

And speaking of silence, is silence music?

45
What is music?

What is music?

This could be a koan asked for eternity.

If you look up the dictionary definition of music, you may read something like this:

music the science or art of ordering tones or sounds in succession, in combination and in temporal relationships to produce a composition having unity and continuity.

It's a dry explanation of something that can render us to the most profound emotions, but with the developments in music in the twentieth century, it is accurate. And those changes were already popping their noisy heads over the fence as early as 1913 when Luigi Russolo writes *The Art of Noises*, a manifesto stating the need for greater variety in musical sounds considering the changes in society and the noises around us. Russolo invents machines that produce the six basic (as he hears them) sounds of life: roars, whistles, whispers, screeches, beatings and wails. That's some life he's leading. Machines are included in music by George Antheil, who uses two airplane propellers in his *Ballet Mécanique*. Unfortunately, but probably not surprisingly, in the first performance at Carnegie Hall, people are blown out of their seats when the propellers are switched on. A newspaper headline of the time reads, 'Terror-stricken women flee cubist music'.

All this leads to music concrète, a style of composing where sounds are recorded from everyday life and used in sound collages. This use of sampling influences musicians from the Beatles all the way through to Frank Zappa, Stevie Wonder and Brian Eno. Contemporary pop music without sampling is simply unimaginable. J.S. Bach is now played on synthesiser, with Wendy Carlos recording *Switched-On Bach* on a Moog, which she has to hit to keep in tune. What would Bartolomeo Cristofori think?

Art is questioning everything, with Hilma af Klint and Mark Rothko and their abstract paintings, Kazimir Malevich and his *Black Square*, and Willem de Kooning and Jackson Pollock with their abstract expressionism. And now music is doing the same.

When you think of the different components of music — pitch, rhythm, dynamics and timbre — all of these aspects are being challenged and extended. With pitch, composers start to experiment with microtones and cluster chords, rhythms are wild and unpredictable, dynamics are impossibly quiet or fiendishly loud, and the timbre, or texture, of music is being taken beyond the traditional possibilities of instruments. Voices scream, cellos are smacked, pianos are scratched and modified with nails and paper, flutes are blown through different holes and horns are taken apart. These extended techniques become part of a musician's world, as if there are no limits to what you can do, or what you must do. Perhaps the ultimate expression of this is Jimi Hendrix burning his electric guitar at the Monterey Festival in 1967.

Rhythm becomes unpredictable, and so does the pulse of music. Aleatoric, or chance, music is developed by composers like Terry Riley in his work 'In C'. Ancient classical music traditions and philosophies from India, Indonesia, China and South-East Asia have a strong influence on rhythm, pitch, pulse and improvisation; we have returned to our roots in the Indus Valley. And now the interpretation of a piece is left almost completely to the musicians — another return, this time to the vagueness of mediaeval neumes pre-Guido of Arezzo and the imprecision of bass lines before figured bass.

Pieces of music become very short (Anton Webern's *Six Bagatelles* last less than a minute each) or beyond-this-lifetime long — John Cage's work for organ 'As Slow As Possible' will last 639 years. We are currently on the twenty-second year of the performance (the first one and a half years were a bar's rest) and have just reached the fourth chord. The organist is ready for a tea break.

Steve Reich and his 'Clapping Music', played solely by clapping hands, shows the minimalism of sound, and that minimalism is taken to its end by John Cage (again) and his work '4'33"', four minutes and thirty-three seconds of ... silence.

But is it music?

What *is* music?

John Cage, '4'33"'
Is music expectation?

...

...

...

Is music expectation?

46

Minimalism meets God

Knock knock.

Who's there?

Knock knock.

Who's there?

Knock knock.

Who's there?

Knock knock.

Who's there?

Philip Glass.

How annoying is that? About as annoying as your coffee cup not fitting in your car's coffee cup holder, but it's one way of illustrating minimalism. Actually, just saying the word 'minimalism' many times over also does the trick. Minimalism

minimalism minimalism minimalism minimalism minimalism
minimalism minimalism …

So you get the picture. Minimalism (and no, we're not
talking about that whole Marie Kondo clearing-out-stuff-that-
doesn't-give-you-joy schtick) in music is a simplification of
pitch, rhythm, dynamics and timbre. So basically, everything we
were talking about in the last chapter, but the complete opposite.
Think white room, white furniture, white pussycat.

So here we are in early 1960s New York. The artist Frank
Stella has already exhibited *The Marriage of Reason and Squalor*,
a work of concentric rectangles and a central straight line
made with black house paint, and given us the equally concise
statement: 'What you see is what you see.' Stella is just one of the
big characters at the beginning of minimalism's life; there's also
Louis Thomas Hardin, who dresses in a Viking outfit and calls
himself Moondog, and someone called Yoko Ono.

Moondog's music is influenced by Native American sounds,
and this in turn affects a young man called La Monte Young.
Young is friends with Yoko Ono, who has recently come to New
York, and Ono agrees to host concerts at her loft apartment.
'Oh no,' you hear the neighbours say. The concerts, attended by
such luminaries as Marcel Duchamp (who left that bicycle wheel
on the stool) and Peggy Guggenheim, are now acknowledged
as the first in proto-minimalistic style. Ono has already been
composing music in a twelve-tone style, but these concerts in
December 1960 focus on conceptual and performance art; for
instance, one piece involves the instruction to draw a straight
line and follow it. La Monte Young's music is already moving

towards a world of sustained sound and silence. In one of his works, Composition 1960 #7, the instruction is 'to be held for a long time' and the piece consists of two notes, a B just below middle C and the F sharp above. Young also instructs that the piece should last for at least four hours.

In this brave new world, there is a lot of stillness and a lot of silence. From this lofty beginning in a loft, composers like Steve Reich, Philip Glass and Terry Riley step along this Zen-like journey, where if something is boring after two minutes, try it for four. If it is still boring, try it for four hours …

Music's journey to minimalism is perhaps best told by the works of Estonian composer Arvo Pärt, who initially creates music in various styles, including collage and twelve-tone technique. He comes to a musical crisis in the late 1960s with the work 'Credo', in which Pärt states his belief in God with screaming atonal music sitting side by side fourteenth-century chanting.

From here, almost nothing for ten years. And then Arvo Pärt composes 'Für Alina', a five-minute work for piano, and it changes music for ever. Pärt has invented a new technique called tintinnabulation, or ringing of little bells, and with this, minimalism moves from the calm, almost removed observing of life to the music of devotion. Minimalism meets God, and although it's not quite holy matrimony, it is holy minimalism. Just as minimalist art strips everything back to the truth of the materials, minimalist music is stripped back to its essence: single sounds. And those sounds become even more distilled with holy minimalism.

Pärt's Orthodox belief and devotion through music is matched by Sir John Tavener in England and Henryk Górecki with his bestselling *Symphony of Sorrowful Songs*.

From composers shouting and telling and demanding, we now have composers who leave more quiet questions than noisy opinions, composers whose music sits calmly in the corner, waiting until the time is right for us to listen.

Galina Grigorjeva, 'In Paradisum'

The music floats out of nothing — it has always been there and it always will be. The high voices hang in the air, waiting, watching, until lower voices come to bring their foundations down to earth. The music stretches into the past and future, hanging, a suspension bridge in the mist flickering in and out of sight and never complete, the line of singers moving forward, individually yet together, across the harbour. And then, on the final fathomless chord, we reach the other side.

Galina Grigorjeva is a Ukrainian composer, currently living in Estonia. She studied in Odesa, St Petersburg and the Estonian National Conservatory under Lepo Sumera, the greatest composer you may never have heard of (check out his Symphony No. 6). The setting of 'In Paradisum' is used in some Christian funeral services as the body is taken out of the church; the Latin text speaks of angels taking us to heaven and leading us to an eternal life.

Grigorjeva's music, written in 2012, is a link to the Orthodox church, with brushes of mediaeval polyphony. A vision of light as substance, light as vibration, the entire rainbow of colour pulsing within and without. Her music is a message from a transparent, sanguine God; here is modesty and deep compassion, the music equivalent of a tiny home. Grigorjeva's teacher, Lepo Sumera, once said, 'Happiness and the renunciation of happiness are to one another so close that they are like one and the same.' Perhaps this is the marrow of holy minimalism.

This music searches for the answer to the ultimate question — what is truth?

47
From post to post

We have listened to so much together, from love songs on a gishgudi four thousand years ago to songs keeping away the Black Death. From music caused by revolutions to music that has pushed revolutions along. From music sung by a single cantor to symphonies of a thousand musicians. We have walked a winter's path with J.S. Bach as he searched for his musical path, we have stood with Clara Schumann as she faces the reality of her existence, we have witnessed Beethoven hearing his final sounds in the Vienna Woods. We have heard solace and chaos, strict rules and experimentation. We have heard music written on dried animal skin and sounds made from electronic sampling, imbedded into a silicon chip.

After all this, what could possibly happen now? How can those four ingredients of music — pitch, rhythm, dynamics and timbre — be changed anymore? Surely, with screams and silence, we have come to an end?

Well, what do you do when you reach the end? You go back to the beginning. Perhaps not to that death-inducing instrument, the aulos, but, yes, back to the chant, the single line, the simple movement from note to note. You go back to the beginning and you look again at harmony, with composers like Hildur Guðnadóttir and Thomas Adès, who have a taste of the mediaeval; you look again at rhythm, with composers like Ross Edwards, Peter Sculthorpe and John Luther Adams, who reveal the pulse of the earth herself. You reckon with the closeness of music, and the intimacy of people now often listening through headphones, with composers like Max Richter. And you listen for new timbres, as computers become one of the most common instruments of our time. From the human voice to skin, gut, wood, bone, metal, plastic and now silicon, music vibrates its way through any medium.

From modern music to postmodern, from classical music to postclassical, pop, jazz and classical music come more and more together in the open octave of sound's delight. Artists like Radiohead, Luke Howard, Queen, Alicia Keys, Lady Gaga, Craig David and Nico Muhly, these classy musicians use classical techniques and an intelligent popular mentality to sing their music to the world.

Nico Muhly, *Keep in Touch*

Nico Muhly takes what is possibly the humblest of string instruments, the viola, and with this piece for viola and prerecorded tape makes it the hero of a supersonic galaxy. Here is an instrument that has been played by the most famous of composers and been at the heart of the most celebrated music, but now we have it on its own, surprised, embarrassed, caught a little underdressed but ultimately fearless.

Muhly is an American composer, born in 1981, who is the definition of a contemporary musician. He studied at Colombia University and the Juilliard School, worked for Philip Glass and Björk, and (so far) has composed operas and film scores, chamber music, orchestral music and concertos, string music for rock bands and indie bands.

This music reworks the chaconne, a musical form first used in South America in the 1500s. The chaconne has a series of chords moving around in a big circle upon which the composer creates variations and layers. Muhly does that with this music, except that these layers are made from sampling, organ, synthesisers, percussion, chanting and chattering, and the viola is pushed to the extremes of its range. We have now travelled from the basilica of chant to the Olympus Mons of music, from the companionship of singing to the quarantining of emotion. And we have a solo instrument desperate to play with others, and yet they remain perpetually remote. The viola bangs its fists on the door of the padded cell, caterwauling, pleading, frantic to get out, desolate in its isolation.

Here is an unerring description of our age of solitude. The music tells us a cautionary tale: we had better keep in touch.

48

Tomorrow

In the time it has taken for you to read this little book, thousands of musicians around the world have written new pieces of music. This brand-new music will contain glimpses of the old, DNA from Enheduanna, Clara Schumann, John Cage and Peter Sculthorpe. And yet, right now, somewhere in the world a young musician is sitting in their bedroom and hearing in their head a completely new sound, a sound with which music will evolve once again. And, just like Enheduanna all those millennia ago, this musician is about to take their own version of a reed stylus and make their mark on a tablet, made now of silicon chips rather than clay. The way music is written is more varied than it ever has been: semiquavers and F-sharps on five-line manuscript, avant-garde representations on blank paper, guitar tabs, melodies recorded into phones, uploaded straight to social media, written into computer software, hummed or forgotten.

Written down so we can play, and listen to, our music tomorrow.

And perhaps, after all this, the single theme that binds all music together is love — love of ourselves, love for each other, love of the things we can know and the things we can never truly know. By writing music, humanity fulfils our ache to know ourselves, to express ourselves so that we can understand and be understood. And love and be loved.

Music we have heard

Athenaios Athenaiou, 'Delphic Paean', c. 128 BCE

Hildegard of Bingen, 'O tu suavissima virga'

Léonin, 'Viderunt omnes'

Guillaume de Machaut, 'Nes que on porroit'

John Dunstaple, 'Veni sancte spiritus'/'Veni creator spiritus'

Maddelena Casulana, 'Morir non puó il mio cuore'

Carlo Gesualdo, 'Moro, lasso, al mio duolo (I Die, Alas, in My
  Suffering)'

Giovanni Pierluigi da Palestrina, 'Stabat mater dolorosa (The
  Sorrowful Mother Standing)'

Giovanni Gabrieli, Sacred Symphonies

Girolamo Frescobaldi, First Book of Canzons

Claudio Monteverdi, 'Pur ti miro (I Gaze Upon You)', *The Coronation of Poppea*

François Couperin, Pieces for Viola da Gamba with Figured Bass

Jean-Baptiste Lully, *The Bourgeois Gentleman*, an orchestral suite

Jean-Philippe Rameau, Pieces for Clavecin (harpsichord) with a Method

Arcangelo Corelli, Twelve Concerti Grossi

Giuseppe Torelli, Violin Concerto in D Minor

J.S. Bach, Brandenburg Concerto No. 6 in B-flat Major, BWV 565

George Frederic Handel, *Water Music*

Christoph Willibald Gluck, 'Che faró senza Euridice? (What Will I Do Without Euridice?)'

Domenico Scarlatti, Sonata for Keyboard in E Major, K380

Johann Stamitz, Symphony in D Major

Joseph Haydn, String Quartet No. 5 in F Minor, Op. 20

Joseph Bologne, Chevalier de Saint-Georges, Symphonie
Concertante in F Major

Maria Theresia von Paradis, 'Morning Song of a Pauper'

Ludwig van Beethoven, Symphony No. 5 in C Minor

Giovanni Paisiello, 'In My Heart I No More Feel the Sparkle of
Youth'

Gioachino Rossini, 'Non piu mesta (No Longer Sad)', from *Cinderella*

Fanny Mendelssohn, Piano Trio in D Minor

Felix Mendelssohn, 'Fingal's Cave'

Franz Schubert, *Die Winterreise (The Winter Journey)*

Clara Schumann, Piano Concerto in A Minor

Giuseppe Verdi, 'Va, pensiero (Chorus of the Hebrew Slaves)', from
Nabucco

Pyotr Ilyich Tchaikovsky, Serenade for Strings

Richard Wagner, 'Siegfried Idyll'

Scott Joplin, 'A Real Slow Drag', from *Treemonisha*

Gustav Mahler, Symphony No. 6 in A Minor

Sir Edward Elgar, 'In the South'

Lili Boulanger, 'D'un soir triste (Of a Sad Evening)'

Dame Ethyl Smyth, 'The March of the Women'

Claude Debussy, 'La cathédrale engloutie (The Submerged
     Cathedral)', Préludes Book I

Arnold Schoenberg, *Two Pieces*, Op. 33

Alban Berg, Violin Concerto

Richard Rodgers and Oscar Hammerstein II, *Oklahoma!*

Bernard Herrmann, *Vertigo*

John Cage, '4'33"'

Galina Grigorjeva, 'In Paradisum'

Nico Muhly, *Keep in Touch*

With thanks

Thank you to the team at ABC Books, and the publisher Mary Rennie. It has been a great pleasure to work with you.

Thank you to the perfect editor, Simone Ford. This is our third book together and I hope there are more out there in the ether.

Thank you to the tall, lean, handsome men – Richard Smart and Martin Buzacott. You have both given me such encouragement in writing, cycling and in life. You are both such good men.

Thank you to Amy Bennett for editing the original podcast scripts and giving excellent feedback. Let's play viola sometime!

Thank you to Juliet Edeson and Sally McLeod for reading the first draft of this little book and giving kind, super smart and positive advice. How did you find the time?

Thank you to the ABC Classic audience for suggesting the original *Pocket Guide* podcast became a book. We really are a family.

And speaking of families, thank you to my Australian family, the Pattersons. Our conversations and dinners and adventures are a constant source of joy.

Thank you to all my students. You teach me more than I can ever teach you.

Happy the dog wants to be included, so thanks, Happy, for your licks and fluff puff-ness.

And my final thanks, as always, to my wife, Charlie. We go forward with ease, joy and glory. How can it get any better than this?

This book is based on the ABC Classic series *Ed's Pocket Guide to Music Through the Ages* which was written by Ed Le Brocq and produced by Amy Bennett, Candice Docker and Sam Emery with original artwork for ABC Classic by Bradley Cook. You can find the episodes on the ABC Classic website and ABC listen app.

Ed Le Brocq is a writer, musician and broadcaster. Previously Ed Ayres, to honour his wife he has taken her family name. Ed studied music in Manchester, Berlin and London, and played professionally in the UK and Hong Kong. Ed is the presenter of ABC Classic's *Weekend Breakfast*.

Ed has written four other books: *Cadence*, about his journey by bicycle from England to Hong Kong with only a violin for company; *Danger Music*, describing his year teaching music in Afghanistan; *Sonam and the Silence*, a children's book about the importance of music; and *Whole Notes*, life lessons in music. Ed's books have been shortlisted for several prestigious awards, including the Prime Minister's Literary Awards and *The Age* Book of the Year.

Ed was born Emma and transitioned just before his fiftieth birthday. Better late than never.